The Girl with the Mermaid Hair

Also by Delia Ephron

Frannie in Pieces

How to Eat Like a Child:
And Other Lessons in Not Being a Grown-up

Teenage Romance:
Or How to Die of Embarrassment

Delia Ephron

The Girl with the Mermaid Hair

HARPER TEEN
An Imprint of HarperCollinsPublishers

To Julia & Richard

Without whom life would be so much paler

HarperTeen is an imprint of HarperCollins Publishers.

The Girl with the Mermaid Hair

www.harperteen.com

Library of Congress Cataloging-in-Publication Data
Ephron, Delia.
The girl with the mermaid hair / Delia Ephron.—1st ed.
p. cm.
Summary: A teenaged girl is obsessed with beauty and perfection until she uncovers a devastating family secret.
ISBN 978-0-06-154260-2 (trade bdg.)
ISBN 978-0-06-154261-9 (lib. bdg.)
[1. Beauty, Personal—Fiction. 2. Perfectionism (Personality trait)—Fiction. 3. Pride and vanity—Fiction. 4. Secrets—Fiction.] I. Title.
PZ7.E7246Gj 2010 2009003061
[Fic]—dc22 CIP
AC

Typography by Amy Toth
10 11 12 13 14 CG/RRDB 10 9 8 7 6 5 4 3 2 1
❖
First Edition

They say that dogs know what's coming. All natural disasters, earthquakes, tornadoes, storms—they feel the earth's tremble, sense electricity in the air before tragedy strikes. Señor had those sensors about the Jamieson family. He knew what was coming before anyone, even before those who would cause it.

The Gift

SUKIE kept track of herself in all reflective surfaces: shiny pots, the windowed doors to classrooms, shop windows, car chrome, knives, spoons. When nothing reflective was conveniently available, she took a selfie. Thank God for selfies. She extended her phone at arm's length, snapped, and with a quick look at the photo was able to scout for trouble spots—eyebrow hairs sticking up, mascara clumps, that sort of thing.

Her vanity and insecurity, huge but in equal proportions, would perhaps have remained stable but for the gift she received the day after the Jamieson family moved into their new house.

Her mom was roaming restlessly around the master bedroom, wading through unpacked cardboard boxes, trying various lamps on the side tables and the bureau, unfurling new duvet covers—which one should she keep?—when she grabbed a pair of scissors and began snipping the tape off a large flat object covered in bubble wrap. It was balanced against the empty bookshelf.

With a few energetic yanks, she stripped off the plastic. "I'm giving you this mirror."

"You are? It's beautiful. I love it." Sukie had never had a full-length mirror.

"It doesn't work in this room, actually it doesn't work in any room in this house, but it's your grandmother's mirror. She admired herself in it, I admired myself in it, I can't stick it back in the basement." Her mother fingered the frame with its two strands of silver twisted together. "It's precious, French from the nineteen forties, but it's old. I don't want to be around anything old, even furniture.

"Go on, you can carry it. Come on, Mikey, help your sister." She directed them as they carted the mirror out of the bedroom and down the hall, letting out little whoops of panic the several times it nearly scraped the freshly painted walls. When Sukie and Mikey had carried the mirror safely through Sukie's bedroom and into her bathroom, and had carefully leaned it against a tiled wall, her mother let out a sigh of relief.

Sukie paraded in a circle in front of the mirror, thrilled that all five feet seven inches of her were reflected. Only yesterday, before school, in order to check out what her bottom half looked like, she'd stood precariously on the sink to view herself through the small oval mirror above it. How short was her tweed skirt, were her knees innocuous or were they fat—her opinion flip-flopped daily—and did the brown flats work better than the red ones, or should she wear boots?

"This mirror will be your best friend and worst enemy," said her mom. She shivered as if a cold wind had just blown through the bathroom, whose window was shut, but Sukie didn't notice because her skin looked especially creamy in her grandmother's mirror, and she had leaned in for a closer look.

Bobo

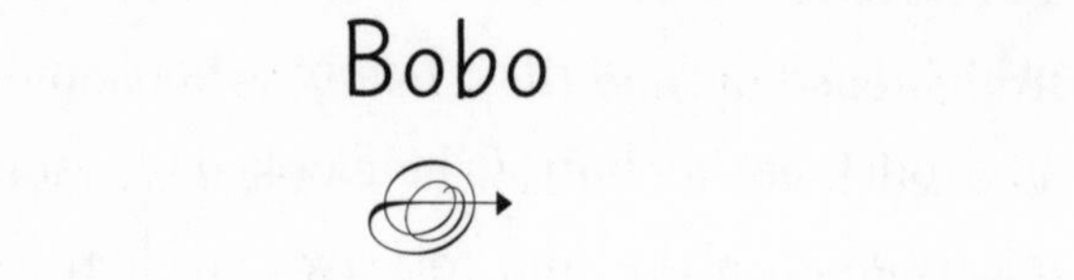

WHEN Sukie tried to impress Bobo, she used a low, breathy voice.

Bobo (his real name was Robert) was the quarterback of the football team at Hudson Glen High. Sukie—who went to Cobweb, a small artsy private school—met him at the mall while buying sunglasses. He bought a wraparound model. Unable to decide among red, gold, or brown frames, Sukie bought nothing. Sometimes making fashion choices paralyzed her. But nothing was more paralyzing than meeting Bobo. He plunked his elbows on the counter, rested his chin in his hands, and watched her try on glasses. She didn't even know him, but it was so cool of him to do that, how cool was it, it was so cool and so confident that Sukie could not continue even to think. It was as if her brain waves had been interfered with—as if an alien had aimed a Disrupter at her. DISRUPT THOUGHTS. DISRUPT THOUGHTS. Then Bobo straightened up, and the straight-up version of his tall, muscled body was a slouch. What was more deeply sexy and appealing than a slouch?

Somehow Sukie had had the presence of mind when he opened the conversation with "Who are you?" to employ her breathy voice. With this voice, "I" is pronounced "Ah," as in, "Ah really don't know."

"Ah really don't know" was a pretty hot answer to just about everything, and for some reason, starting a sentence with "Ah" caused her voice to drop an octave and sound phenomenally sophisticated and blasé.

"You don't know *who* you are?" said Bobo. "Well, I don't know either, but *how* you are is fine."

Fine didn't only mean fine like okay or not having the flu, it clearly meant that Sukie had passed a magnificently important attractiveness test. Bobo smiled at her. His smile snuck over his face. *Like dawn breaking*, she wrote in her journal, a red hardcover book with lined pages that Sukie filled nightly with every thought and experience that she deemed worthy of recording. *Wider and wider his smile grew until his eyes crinkled up and his white teeth sparkled in the fluorescent mall lights, or perhaps that's what I imagined, because all I could think was "I want to rip my clothes off."*

Such a thought had never occurred to her before.

Later they'd had Diet Cokes with several of Bobo's friends, and Sukie sat there saying nothing but feeling that she was the luckiest girl in the world and hoping that someone from Cobweb would pass by and see her. When they were leaving, and after Bobo had programmed her number into his cell, he put his hand on her back and said, "I really like your body-fat ratio."

Sukie didn't quite know what to make of that, but it caused her to spend an hour naked with her back to her grandmother's mirror while she held a smaller mirror up in front of her and moved it around to see what was so great, what in the world was he talking about.

Bobo.

She practiced his name in the mirror, watching her lips. They narrowed with each B sound. Bo-bo. Bo-bo. She pouted and popped the name out that way. Bo-bo. Bo-bo. It was impossible to smile while saying his name, and this concern caused a small vertical crease to appear between her eyebrows. Whenever that happened, whenever a distressing thought crossed her mind while she gazed at her reflection, she took a deep breath and assumed her "mirror face," one that was relaxed and betrayed no emotion whatsoever. A face, in short, that didn't exist except when she looked in the mirror.

Señor

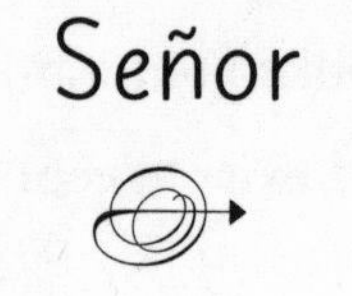

BOBO hadn't phoned or texted. Two weeks had gone by.

"Is your cell in your lap?" asked her mom.

"Yes," said Sukie.

"Put it upstairs in your room."

Sukie's hand tightened around the phone. "I won't talk on it."

"But we're at dinner," said her mom. "And every time I look up, you're sneaking a peek. It's rude. You might be addicted to it."

"I'm not addicted."

"She's probably not addicted," said her dad.

"I think she's addicted," said her mom.

"Come on," said her dad. "Hey, what do you think,

Señor? Does my darling daughter have a problem?"

Sukie, her mom, and her younger brother, Mikey, turned to their dog, Señor, who sat at the head of the table.

When they all looked to see what Señor thought—and it was not the first time—Señor didn't bark. He wasn't a trick dog. He didn't bark once for yes and twice for no. And he wasn't a talking dog, there's no such thing. Medium-sized with a thick white coat, short pointed ears that were rosy pink inside, and a long graceful snout, Señor had powerful silent communication skills and an incredibly intimidating manner. He never licked anyone. None of that grateful happy kissing for Señor. No one had ever seen him roll over for a tummy rub, and his tail, which curled up over his back, did not wag. No one had ever seen him fetch his red rubber ball either. Every so often Mikey threw it for the amusement of watching Señor ignore it. "Is this your dog?" people would ask when they entered the house, even though Señor was clearly the Jamiesons' dog, what else would he be doing there, but there was something about his elegance, his reserve, the way he observed without moving a muscle that made people question whether he was a pet, anyone's pet. When one night he climbed into the chair at the head of the table, no one questioned it. Sukie's dad simply slid his place setting out of Señor's way and over to the long side of the rectangular table next to Sukie's. Her mom, at the other end, did likewise so that she sat next to Mikey. Señor, at the head, had the only chair with arms.

Did Sukie have a phone addiction? The family awaited Señor's verdict. His watchful gray eyes did not narrow, a good sign, and his mouth dropped open slightly, revealing small, even bottom teeth and the tip of his pink tongue.

"No," said Sukie tentatively. "No, I don't. No problem. I'm fine!" She jumped up and hugged Señor, gunking up her red sweater with white hairs. It was Señor's shedding season.

"Look at you," said her mom. "I'll get the lint roller." She put down her fork and stood up.

"For God's sake, Felice, we just sat down," said her dad.

"Mom," said Sukie, "Señor thinks you should stay."

Mikey slid down in his seat so his eyes were level with the tabletop.

"I don't want to eat," said her mom. "I'm five pounds up. I am. Five pounds." She struggled to control herself, blinking rapidly to bat back the tears, flapping her arms. Whenever her mom had a flapping fit—and they were not infrequent—Sukie thought she looked like a baby bird desperately wanting to fly but unable to take off.

"Get the lint thing," her dad said.

"Yes, thanks, Mom," said Sukie. "I could really use it."

"Don't look at my backside. Do you promise? Do you swear?"

Sukie's dad kicked Sukie under the table, and Sukie kicked Mikey. All three said, "Promise."

Her mom left the room with her hands crossed behind her, forming a little shield so they couldn't see her fanny.

Fortunately her mom was taking her overweight fears to a spa for a week. *Mom, leaving for a week. Thank God,* Sukie wrote in her journal.

Her mom was pretty scattered when Sukie helped her pack. They were in her parents' bedroom, the suitcase was open, and Mikey was programming the remote on the new flat-screen TV. Ever since he was five years old—he was eight now—Mikey had provided tech support for the family. The bedroom was "in progress." Fabric swatches draped a flock of pillows on the bed. There were two love seats on approval—"Both will probably be returned," her mom had said.

Sukie was running through a mental checklist. "Don't forget your bathing suit." She held up her mom's black one-piece, a sleek, glamorous item with artfully placed cutouts, something she'd told Sukie she'd graduated to. "You begin with bikinis," she'd said. "After you give birth, you find these peekaboo suits, and then finally, when it all goes to hell—your body, that is—you buy a plain, dreary tank that you could swim the English Channel in."

While her mom stared blankly, Sukie packed the suit.

"I won't need it."

"Of course you will. There'll be a Jacuzzi and a swimming pool, right?"

"You know," said her mom, eyeing a fabric swatch. "I'm partial to that pale green. It's the color of a daiquiri." Sukie's mom took the bathing suit out of the suitcase and put it back in the drawer.

The Text

SUKIE held her phone at arm's length and snapped.

A difficult thing, taking a selfie. Sometimes her face came out lopsided or only a piece of it showed. The photo she took today was critical, because she was about to enter Mr. Vickers's AP English class, where she would present her report, "Ophelia: Angel or Fool?" For ten minutes she would be standing in front of the class.

She was tired, although she was pleased to see from the selfie that no one could tell. She'd gotten to bed at two in the morning, three hours later than usual. After completing her homework—a take-home test for AP math, her English essay, fifty pages of reading about the Civil War for AP history, and a chapter for zoology on the scientific value of fruit flies, in addition to preparing for her debate question (con: Dubai, an environmental disaster) and taking a flute lesson (she'd eaten dinner in the car on the way over—ham and Swiss with lettuce and tomato on oat-nut bread and a bottle of water) . . . after all that, which was an ordinary day in her life, she'd gone into the bathroom to brush her teeth. Hours later she finally turned off the light. Her grandmother's mirror had proved compelling.

It had a wrinkle in it—not an actual wrinkle, but because it was old, Sukie assumed, the glass appeared to wrinkle at approximately her waist level and made her waist appear smaller. This was fascinating and flattering, and she had viewed her waist from several angles to confirm it. She'd decided to rehearse her essay in front of the mirror, incorporating a back-and-forth stroll (rejected) and arm gestures (kept). Then while surfing the web she had come upon a site for would-be models that catalogued face and feature types. It had names for eyes like "almond," "button," "egg," "half-moon" (which had less to do with shape than with the lids that sat low on the eyes like shades). Sukie, racing from the computer to the mirror, was pleased to conclude that her type was "lake," clearly the most desirable. Her eyes were large, wide set, and thickly lashed. They had allure and suggested depth of feeling and, she suspected, even passion.

Her grandmother's mirror had a slight tint. Reflected in it, Sukie's eyes, a warm cocoa color like her dad's, appeared green. Not emerald, which would be thrilling, but a dark olive. Still, that was so much more interesting than brown that Sukie thanked the mirror and blew it a kiss.

She had always wished for blue-green eyes—the color of sea in a fairy-tale book, a sea that a mermaid swam in. Sukie had mermaid hair, a long wavy tangle of blond that fell below her shoulders. In the antique mirror, her hair appeared exceptionally lustrous. She pushed it around, threaded her fingers through it, grabbed a hunk that lay on her shoulder and pulled it forward to make eye contact as if to say, What is this, I'd forgotten all about you. Then she tossed it back over her shoulder as if her thick golden hair were nothing but a nuisance instead of a mane worthy of worship.

What had really kept her up late, however, was her nose, her most arresting feature. She was dreadfully self-conscious about it, and after studying nose varieties on the web such as "Greek" (a straight and narrow nose, the most desirable) and "Miss Piggy" (the least), she decided that her own category was "ramp." In fact, her prominent nose (inherited from her mother), while finely chiseled on the sides, did have a flatness from top to tip. Why this peculiarity made her more attractive rather than less is a mystery. Everyone knows but no one can explain why the unconventional, even a flaw, can make a person more beautiful.

Nevertheless, about this Sukie was clueless. She hated her nose. "Ramp," she said, despairing at her reflection. "I have ramp." By confirming this news, was the mirror being her best friend or her worst enemy? Sukie couldn't decide which.

Mikey stuck his head in the door at that moment, his face in a crumple, which Sukie knew meant "I'm scared, I can't sleep."

"Okay," she said. "Just for *Jeopardy!*" and he dove onto the bed.

Sukie taped *Jeopardy!* every day and watched before sleep. For her *Jeopardy!* was a lullaby. She beat the TV contestants that night as she always did, even being preoccupied with "ramp," even not phrasing two answers as questions on purpose so that Mikey would get to say, "I'm sorry, that's incorrect." The Final Jeopardy question was "the South American country farthest west." "What is Peru?" said Sukie. She was the only one who got it. The contestants all wrote "What is Ecuador?" She and Mikey did their special pinkie lock, she shooed him back to his room, and she made one last notation in her journal—*I love my mirror*—before drifting off to sleep.

As she entered Mr. Vickers's classroom, Sukie tried to glide as if she were wearing skates and the floor were ice. This gliding walk—graceful, eye-catching—fortified her with confidence.

Cobweb classrooms had tables, not desks. Round tables that seated six. "Cobweb is about the three C's: creativity, community, and culture," the principal announced every year at the first meeting, Cobweb's cozy word for an all-school assembly. Sitting together at tables was supposed to foster a friendly, cooperative atmosphere.

"That's all a crock," said Sukie's dad. "No one's trying to get along, they're trying to get ahead. That's America."

"Then why do you and Mom send me to Cobweb?"

"So you'll get into a good college. Just don't take that bunk seriously."

Sukie sat at the middle table between Fleur Ames and Denicia Hays. Denicia was blowing a bubblegum bubble that popped as Sukie glided toward her. Denicia took the gum out of her mouth and used it to mop up stray gum bits on her face. "Hi," said Sukie, while she thought, I would rather die than do that in public. Fleur had flopped her head down on the table and appeared to be napping. If she keeps that up, thought Sukie, the cheek she's lying on will eventually droop lower than the other. Always sleep on your back, her mother had advised. It was a rule Sukie lived by, although sometimes when she awoke in the morning, she found herself on her side. Fleur was clearly someone who didn't think about the future in any serious way, and not simply because her face was going to be lopsided. Fleur's nails were at least two inches long, so long that they curved. It was practically impossible for her to hold a pencil or type on a computer, not to mention the annoyingly loud clattering as she attempted to hit the keys.

Obviously Fleur was not being raised properly. Were her parents even home?

When Sukie pulled her chair out, it banged into

Frannie, who was doodling at the table behind. "Sorry," mumbled Sukie. Frannie shrugged.

One of the most important things in the world, Sukie's dad had told her, was to look someone straight in the eye when you spoke to them. With Bobo, Sukie had been so nervous that she'd focused on a mole on his neck. On the debate team or when she had to read a report as she did today, she would force herself to make eye contact with her audience to "drive the points home," as her dad put it. But she never looked Frannie Cavanaugh in the eye, no matter what.

Frannie's father had died last spring, and Sukie kept thinking that she should say, "I'm sorry about your dad." Sukie's mom had even asked, "Did you tell Frannie that you're sorry?" and Sukie had said, "Duh," like she really needed reminding about that, but she'd never actually said word one to Frannie about her dad. Every day she'd think, I'll do it today. Then she'd go home and say to herself, I'll do it tomorrow for sure. But she never did, and now it was too late. The whole idea of it, losing your dad, didn't seem real. If she didn't acknowledge it, maybe it didn't happen at all. Maybe it couldn't happen to *her.* Nothing truly horrible had ever happened to Sukie, and she wanted to keep it that way.

To understand everything that frightened her about Frannie's father's death, Sukie would have to delve deep into her heart. Digging—unearthing painful truths, exploring subtlety, reveling in the complexity of emotion—was not her nature. Although that could change. She was fifteen years old. Nothing was set in stone.

Perhaps she was simply worried that Frannie would tell her that it was unspeakably rude not to have said, "I'm sorry about your dad." Sukie didn't like thinking about that. She didn't like to acknowledge any situation in which she was less than perfect.

Sukie also felt sorry for Frannie because of her hair. Frannie's hair was a big frizz. It didn't move. The most important thing about hair—Sukie had given this a lot of thought—was that it should move.

"Hey, everyone, listen up. This is important." Mr. Vickers waved a sheaf of papers. "Fleur, wake up, get some exercise and hand these out for me, thank you very much. Everyone should give this notice to your parents. They'll go bat shit if you don't."

Mr. Vickers was always using language that, in Sukie's opinion, had no place in school. And for some reason, he had cracked himself up, like what he'd said was really amusing. Sukie read the large type at the top of the flyer. "Prepare for college. Find out what your child needs in order to get into the best school."

What was funny about that?

She unzipped the small compartment on the side of her backpack. As she slipped the notice in, she felt the phone's sleek surface. It vibrated. She jerked it out into her lap.

Bobo. A text from Bobo.

She slipped the college notice back out and opened it so that she would appear to be reading it while instead she read the text from Bobo: ROLL ME OVER.

Roll me over?

Sukie felt her blood rush in every direction that blood could rush.

Roll me over.

She didn't even know what it meant.

But it meant something hot.

Although this could just be hello. A provocative hello for sure. But it didn't feel like hello. It felt almost, but not quite, but maybe, nasty.

What should she say back?

"The college meeting is two weeks from Wednesday. I know your parents are concerned about your futures, and even though there's no reason to panic, after all you're sophomores, you don't take your college boards till next year . . ." Vickers droned on while Sukie sat there, thumbs poised, ready to tap. What was called for? "Hi 2 U." No that's dumb. Stupid. A big nothing. Roll me over. Hmm. Sukie tapped: W-H-E-N W-E K-N-O-W E-A-C-H O-T-H-E-R B-E-T-T-E-R.

Dorky. That was dorky. Or was it flirty? Too flirty? Yes. Beyond flirty? Sukie hit the delete and held it down.

WHEN WE KNOW EACH OTHER BETTER

WHEN WE KNOW EACH OTHER BETTE

WHEN WE KNOW EACH OTHER BETT

WHEN WE KNOW EACH OTHER BET

WHEN WE KNOW EACH OTHER BE

WHEN WE KNOW EACH OTHER B

WHEN WE KNOW EACH OTHER

WHEN WE KNOW EACH OTHE

WHEN WE KNOW EACH OTH

WHEN WE KNOW EACH OT

WHEN WE KNOW EACH O

WHEN WE KNOW EACH

WHEN WE KNOW EAC

WHEN WE KNOW EA

WHEN WE KNOW E

WHEN WE KNOW

WHEN WE KNO

WHEN WE KN

WHEN WE K

WHEN WE

WHEN W

WHEN

Mr. Vickers's hand slapped down in front of her so close she saw his lifeline. Sukie hit send.

"Hand it over," said Vickers.

"I sent 'when.'" The words popped out unbidden as Sukie confronted the horror.

"When what?"

"When nothing."

The class laughed. Sukie tried to laugh, but her face was twitching. She'd offered to—what? She didn't know what she'd offered Bobo, but she'd definitely agreed to whatever he'd asked. If he was asking. Was he asking? What was he asking? She held on to the phone.

"I'll give it back to you after school." Vickers tugged at her cell.

That night she wrote in her journal, *At that moment I was in the ocean clinging for life to a small boat. Realizing I didn't have the strength to hold on any longer, I felt my grip loosen and my fingers fail.*

Vickers walked to the front of the class, unsnapped the buckle on his battered leather briefcase, and dropped the phone in.

Issy

"OKAY, Sukie," said Vickers. "Now that you're light as a feather, phone-free, as they say. Come on, upsy. Time for Shakespeare. Let's hear about Ophelia."

Sukie dragged herself to the front of the class.

She forgot to do a little twist at the waist to force herself ramrod straight, and she could barely make out the words on the page through watery eyes. With one tap of the thumb she'd blown it with Bobo. Maybe. For sure. For sure maybe. She forgot to swing out her arm to go with "Ophelia was muddled, muddled by love," and omitted a flip of the hands up with a gentle push forward to underscore "Think about this: If Ophelia had had options as a woman, would she have ever gone haywire?" When she spoke of Ophelia, dumped by Hamlet and desolate, climbing a tree, inching herself onto a branch, and falling to her death, everyone in the class mistook the tears in her voice for performance. For a second, to collect herself, she glanced up, and whose eye did she catch but Frannie's, the sole person about whom she harbored a horrible guilt. She lowered her eyes and uttered the last words barely audibly, "Did Ophelia overreact?"

Mr. Vickers clapped. "Bravo. Beautifully presented and with such feeling."

Sukie sank into her seat, relieved that she would get another A.

The instant the bell rang, she knocked Denicia out of the way. "Move, move." Sukie barged up. "Mr. Vickers—"

"You'll get it after school." He turned his attention to Ethan, who wanted to change his topic. Ethan never liked his topics. Sukie had been in school with Ethan since the first grade, and there had never been one single assignment for which they were supposed to pick a topic when Ethan had stuck with the topic he'd picked. "Boring," she told Ethan, sticking her sour face into his.

"You're done here, Sukie," said Vickers. "But, you know, you might have an addiction to your cell phone. Give it some thought. You kids are all phone addicts," he bellowed at the backs of students filing out. "Consider a twelve-step program. *Adiós* till next time."

It was one thing if your mom called you an addict, she had a right, but your teacher? In Sukie's opinion, Vickers was seriously out of control. And weren't his clothes a curiosity? Mostly he favored thick, woolly pullover sweaters. The one he was wearing today changed colors in a loud and utterly random pattern. Had someone knitted it blindfolded? Perhaps he'd selected it blindfolded. Perhaps he'd been turned loose in Harry's, the local men's store, where practically everything was plaid, wool, or flannel, and, in a kind of blindman's bluff game, had had to buy whatever he crashed into.

These hostile thoughts didn't bring her phone back, but they were comforting.

"Did something awful happen?" Fleur waylaid her in the locker room and struggled to suppress the thrill. The combination of Sukie and disaster gave her heart a happy flutter, but Sukie was too crazed to notice.

"Bobo," said Sukie. It would be at least two hours

and twenty-two minutes before she could correct her mistake. This was perhaps the seventeenth time she'd computed the hours until she could get her phone back. *My mind was a blubber,* she wrote later in her journal. During lunch period at the Educating Girls Globally meeting, Sukie accidentally put her mascara into her lunch bag, tossed it in the trash, and had to fish it out. When she did reclaim her phone from Vickers, should she text OOPS MISTAKE to Bobo? Or HO, HO, HO, meaning her last message was a big joke? Or would he not even know what she was referring to since she'd sent her previous message six hours earlier?

She relived the incident with a different outcome. Vickers's hand slapped down and Sukie's thumb did not reflexively hit SEND. It lay there obediently.

"I said, 'Is Bobo your dog?'"

Sukie was so preoccupied, she'd forgotten Fleur. "My dog's name is Señor. Bobo is the quarterback at Hudson Glen." God, how could Fleur not know? "The star quarterback."

"Shoot, damn these lockers." Fleur slammed her locker door, it bounced back, she slammed it again and examined her middle finger. "Twenty dollars down the drain. Don't anyone move, there it is."

She snatched something off the ground and showed it to Sukie. A two-inch fake nail painted a sparkly lavender.

"He texted me."

Fleur tried to fit the nail back onto her middle finger.

"Bobo," Sukie reminded her loudly to get the conversation back on track and attract some admiration from someone somewhere. Moira was jumping around while she tugged at too-small tights in an effort to get them up to her waist. Autumn was reading *Death of a Salesman* and mouthing the words to her part. Frannie, stretched out on a bench with a pencil balanced across her forehead, removed the pencil and shot her friend Jenna a look that was quite possibly amused.

"He plays football." Sukie trumpeted the news again.

"Who has nail glue?" said Fleur, disappearing into a maze of lockers. Frannie rolled off the bench and pulled her feet up under her just in time not to crack her head on the cement floor. She and Jenna walked away, leaving Sukie alone in her lacy raspberry-colored bra, her best bra for creating breast envy.

After school, as soon as she rescued her phone from Vickers's grimy paws, she rushed out of his classroom and checked for messages. There was one. PIZZA. PICK YOU UP AT 5, DADDY.

Maybe it was a good thing that Bobo hadn't replied. It was possible he hadn't seen her WHEN, and therefore her new message could follow right behind it. Although this was unlikely. If he was anything like anyone else, he was punching his phone nonstop, sending messages flying at any opportunity. Still, he was an athlete. He couldn't text on the field.

Carefully, slowly, she punched in another message for Bobo. J-U-S-T K-I-D-D-I-N-G. After obsessing for hours, "just kidding" was the best she could come up with. She slumped against the wall, exhausted. I am so uncreative, she thought. I'm practically a blob.

Afterward, studying in the library, she kept her phone clutched in her hand (risking another confiscation), praying for it to vibrate. "Sure," she told Mrs. Dintenfass, and when Mrs. Dintenfass said, "I knew you would. I'll put you down, then," Sukie had no idea what Mrs. Dintenfass had asked her or what she was being put down for. Normally able to speed-read and retain twenty-five pages in ten minutes—she'd timed it with Mikey on the stopwatch—she found herself spacing out on a paragraph about epiparasites and endoparasites, starting it again and again, retaining nothing.

Standing outside, waiting for her dad to get her, Sukie double- and triple-checked her phone. Was it working? Her skirt was off-kilter. The back zipper had moved all the way over to the side—it had a tendency to self-shift. Did her way of walking contribute to this? She hadn't yet figured it out, but usually she kept better track of the problem. Finally she saw the flat top of the Bronco looming. She climbed into the backseat, letting Mikey have the front, a rarity. "Did Mom leave okay?"

"She forgot her Fiji water. She phoned from the car," said her dad.

"What were you supposed to do about that?"

"Good question."

"What about the building?"

"I'm waiting for them to counter."

He launched into the drawbacks of adjustable versus fixed-rate mortgages. Sukie kept her eyes on her phone, hoping that a message would surface. *I'll count to ten and then it will come.* Silently counting, she didn't hear a word her dad said. "You've got a good business head," he told her, pleased to fill the air with his knowledge, getting confused as he often did: His daughter's listening to his brilliance automatically conferred brilliance on her. Even though she wasn't listening. She was barely giving the appearance of listening, but how could he know? He was driving and she was sitting behind him.

When they had parked and Mikey had raced ahead into Clementi's Pizza Parlor, her dad said, "Good thing your mom isn't here, she'd be all flipped out about the calories in mozzarella."

"Omigod!" Sukie shrieked. "Cheese! I ate cheese!"

They laughed together, a cozy feeling.

"Should we tell her we ate here?"

"No," said Sukie.

"Where should we say we ate?"

"At home. You cooked."

"What did I make?" he asked.

"Tuna sandwiches."

"Great. I like that."

Sukie shook her head, letting her hair fluff out and settle. She did that when she felt especially good, as she did right now talking to her dad in a grown-up way, which gave her a momentary break from her agitation about Bobo and the sense, based on nothing except the security of being with her dad, that Bobo would text her. Any minute now. He'd probably been at football practice.

"She drives me a little crazy," said her dad.

"Me too," said Sukie.

Her dad took out his money clip, refolded his bills, and clipped them again. He always did that when he was thinking.

"Maybe it will calm her down."

"What?" said Sukie. "The spa?"

He opened the door to Clementi's. "After you, Your Gorgeousness."

Sukie loved walking into restaurants with her dad, because people glanced up and got stuck. Yes, up they glanced and then couldn't tear their eyes away from Sukie's tall, handsome dad, who oozed confidence. Sukie knew she was pretty striking too. A few of the lingering looks were directed at her. She imagined what people were thinking. "What perfect father-daughter specimens." No. Something less scientific. Exactly what escaped her.

Isabella, the hostess, escorted them to a booth (never a table) and personally served Sukie's dad his usual, Bombay on the rocks with a twist, checking with Sukie and Mikey about their orders. "Diet Coke and Seven Up, right?"

"And three glasses of tap," her dad added, which was the way he always ordered water.

Isabella even set up the little pizza stand. That was what they always had, the margherita.

"Move over, buddy," her dad told Mikey so Isabella could join them for a minute. Issy had studied film at the New School in New York City and was working at Clementi's while she considered her options. "I found a water bug in my kitchen as big as this." She pointed to a dinner roll in the bread basket.

"Next time you've got a bug to kiss," said Sukie's dad, "call Mikey."

"Me?" said Mikey. "I'm not kissing a bug."

"Did I say kiss? I meant kill."

"I'm not killing one either," said Mikey.

Everyone laughed, even the people in the booth behind them.

"Do you like pepperoni?" Her dad addressed the table across the way. "I don't know. I don't get it."

"Me either," said the wife. "See, I'm not the only one." She punched her husband in the arm.

The husband pretended to be injured and then offered Sukie's dad some pickled peppers. Sukie's dad tried one and passed them on to the booth behind, and pretty soon he had all three tables in a three-way conversation about pizza toppings.

Sukie loved to watch her dad operate. That's what he called it. Once at Cones, when he'd offered to pay for a woman's sprinkles (a woman they'd never met before), the woman said to Sukie, "Your father makes everything more fun, doesn't he?" As soon as they'd left the store, she reported the compliment to her dad, and he whispered (so her mom and Mikey couldn't hear), "I'm a real operator." Clearly this was information he could entrust only to Sukie.

Being a towering six feet four inches, he cocked his head down to listen, smiling as people told him stuff, as if their confidences cheered his heart. "Love it," he said sometimes for no reason that Sukie could figure, simply because he was enjoying himself. "How's your back, any better?" "What'd you do about the bee infestation?" "Did you quit your job?" "Still scuba diving?" Warren Jamieson remembered what people told him weeks, even months earlier.

"How's Richie?" he asked.

Isabella sighed, "I may give up men."

"Already?" said her dad.

"I'm twenty-two."

"What happened?" asked Sukie.

"Oh, I don't know. You know . . ." Issy scrunched up her face.

In Sukie's opinion only a woman with an excellent bone structure like Isabella's could scrunch up her face and still look cute. On the face description website, which Sukie had committed to memory, the worst bone structure was called "pudding" and the best was called "landscape." Issy certainly had "landscape": a determined line to her chin, sweet curves in her cheeks with hollows under them, a perfectly proportioned nose—"ski slope" made more flatteringly severe by a touch of "Greek." Sukie sighed over the paleness of Issy's skin. Only the barest blush of pink in her cheeks indicated that she was not dead, her complexion being nearly as white as the cameo Sukie had inherited from her great-aunt. Issy was small and delicate. "Drop me and I break," she'd once laughed to Sukie and her dad, which Sukie thought was the cleverest way to talk about oneself. She'd tried the line in the mirror later. Since Sukie was tall and strong with arms and legs muscled from playing tennis, she had to admit that the line worked only if you had the looks to go with it. Isabella's short hair, currently dyed pink (the color changed frequently), hadn't been chopped with hedge clippers, but if that had turned out to be true, no one would have been surprised. She stabbed it with clips. It stood up every which way.

Issy grabbed a lock of hair and reclipped it as she shivered over the memory of picking up a bottle of Coors and uncovering the giant bug. Her hands zigzagged as she recounted the bug's skitter out of the kitchen and through her living room. Sukie became transfixed by Issy's tiny wrists.

Her dad caught one of Isabella's wrists. With his thumb and index finger he was able to circle it nearly twice. "You're as tiny as a baby bird," he said.

Sukie gasped. "I was just thinking that. That's so weird. We were having exactly the same thought at the same time."

Her dad smiled his famous smile. Sukie called it his famous smile because it was good enough to be on a can of peas or a box of oatmeal or a jar of popcorn, to name a few of the products Sukie had seen where a man's smiling face assured you that this was the one to buy.

Isabella, she noticed, remained fixated on her wrist. If she'd been wearing a watch, you'd think she was having trouble reading the dial. She sure is spacey, thought Sukie. If her wrist confuses her, she might take years figuring out her options.

Issy slid her wrist free of Sukie's dad as if she were slipping off a bracelet, and stood up to return to her duties.

"If you get any more bugs, let me know." He gave Issy his card. "I've got a good guy I can send out."

Isabella's exit and her dad's carrying his drink to the bar to chat, which Sukie knew was a way to check the score of the Giants game and distribute a few more of his business cards, created a void that Bobo rushed to fill. She started to beat up on herself again about her lame response. She checked her cell. No message.

I am so unoriginal. Sukie recorded the dreaded feeling in her journal that night while Señor snored next to her, taking up most of the bed. "Do you agree, Señor?"

Señor twitched, indicating that he was dreaming.

Unoriginal. She hoped it wasn't true but despaired that it was.

She collected stuffed penguins. Was that unoriginal too? Was lining them up in a row on the windowsill a conventional way to display them? They all had names.

She'd started with A, Anton, and worked her way down the alphabet to M, Marshmallow, a very small bird with a yellow bow. Sometimes she thought of them as friends, sometimes as audience. Tonight they sat in judgment. Over their furry black heads the moon was bright white, so low in the sky that it might roll off a rooftop, and perfectly round. A storybook moon, she thought. A wishing moon. She wondered if that thought was especially original; probably not. Could she fake being original, or was that something you couldn't fool anyone about? *I wish I knew what everyone thought of me, really,* she wrote. *No, I take that back.*

Sukie scooted down to the foot of the bed to get off without disturbing Señor.

In her grandmother's mirror she assessed herself, not trying to appear up or down, glittery or punk, icy or blazing. This was a serious and strict appraisal. Impartial, as if that were possible. Sukie, somber, stood arms akimbo, feet apart and front facing. (Not that clever stance her mom had taught her, where the feet are together with one foot slightly in front. "A model's pose." Her mother had demonstrated. "Try to remember to use it when you're being photographed because you'll look"—her mother lowered her voice conspiratorially—"so much thinner.")

Sukie's mom hadn't called. Maybe the spa was one of those ashrams where you meditated for hours and weren't allowed to do anything normal like use a phone. Sukie had forgotten to ask.

She bore in on her reflection. "What does everyone think of me really?" Her lip curled, snarling at her.

Is that what they think?

She assumed her mirror face, the ultimate in blandness, but in the reflection her upper lip continued to twitch. She tapped it with her finger, stop misbehaving, but it snaked right back up again.

What does Bobo think of me?

My hair might have blinded him, she decided. To what? To whatever that lip of hers was snarling at. Sukie did feel that her hair was spectacular, and right now she calmed herself by pushing some of it from one side of her head to the other.

"Hi there." Sukie evaluated a variety of waves and smiles, imagining that she was greeting Bobo. "Hi *there.*" She put the emphasis on the second word, how unexpected was that? She tried a brief signaling wave, where her hand popped up for a second, then tried a broader, windshield-wiper move. She left the bathroom and walked back in, swishing her hips, swiveled to the mirror, and flipped her hand up, "Hey." Perched on the edge of the tub, legs crossed, she practiced interested looks—sultry and penetrating, concerned and warm, skeptical. Oddly, she favored skeptical, which involved a slight smirk and some eye narrowing.

She tried the whole thing all over again wearing boots. Just black leather knee-high boots and underwear.

Should she send another message?

Sukie recalled a movie she'd seen where a guy left about fifty messages for a girl—trying to correct a previous message, and then correct that previous message, and the next and the next and so on and so forth—until he was worse than an idiot, he was a lunatic. Sukie didn't want to be an idiot or a lunatic. Well, she might already be an idiot and a lunatic, but she didn't want Bobo to know it.

Señor stretched, stiffening his legs. With one jump, he stood up on all fours and blinked.

"You're right. You are so right. A bath. I need to take a hot bath. Thanks, Señor." Only a hot bath could calm the jumps, her special word for the way her body felt when she was agitated.

While the tub filled, she strode around the bathroom in her boots and underwear. "Where are the documents, Jim?" she said for no reason whatsoever and saluted her reflection. She scrunched up her face and said to the mirror, "Oh, you know," in Issy's scratchy voice. But unlike Issy's darling scrunch, Sukie's face simply wrinkled. After lighting two candles, vanilla scented, and shutting off the bathroom lights, she stripped and lowered herself slowly into the hot bath; then, lying flat on her back, she submerged just enough for her hair to float around her.

Her cell rang.

Sukie shot up, splashing water out of the tub.

Silence. Was there no call? Had she imagined it?

She waited a moment in case there had been a call and it had failed. Then the person would hit redial.

Nothing.

Sukie reclined, again submerging only deep enough for her hair to float around her. This pastime was her favorite, an invention, maybe even an act of originality. She'd given it a name: the mermaid float.

The Mirror

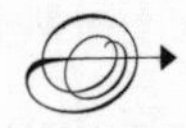

"TAKE a book. A book. B-O-O-K." Mr. Vickers shoved them into his students' arms as they walked into class. "These books are not made with recycled paper," he told Ethan, who was handing out flyers about pollution in the Hudson Glen reservoir. "Are people who recycle more sensitive than those who don't? Are they less likely to beat their children? Here, Sukie, Frannie, take copies of this magnificent novel." He turned and wrote on the board in his weird slanting handwriting, the letters seemingly flattened by a stiff wind: *Madame Bovary* by Gustave Flaubert. "I'll tell you whom this book is for. Lovesick girls and boys who watch porn on the web. And I'll tell you why. Because Madame Bovary lived for her fantasies. She lived so much for her fantasies that reality could never measure up. Whatever happened was a disappointment."

Sukie felt an instant kinship with Madame Bovary.

While not stuck in a convent as Madame Bovary was as a teenager, but trapped nevertheless in a brand-new development home with deep-pile carpeting blanketing room after room like sand in the Sahara, Sukie wondered about her own fantasies. Could Bobo the person ever measure up to the Bobo of her dreams? Perhaps it was just as well that he hadn't texted her again.

I guess he's over. I hate this weight on my chest, she wrote that night in her journal. She put a little arrow and inserted *sad* between *this* and *weight,* then crossed out *chest* and put *breast. I hate this sad weight on my breast.* She blacked out the entire sentence with a solid crisscross of horizontal and vertical lines so that no one could ever see through the crossout. Her inability to express herself poetically piled despair upon despair.

He is gone. Believe it.

"If only I could believe it," she told Señor, "he would turn up again."

Why was that true?

Sukie knew with a sudden and rare clarity that it was. She was lying on her bed with her journal and a pile of different-colored Sharpies. (She liked to switch depending on what she was expressing—everything about Bobo was written in deep purple.) She had bitten into a crisp juicy apple and wondered if the bite and the thought were connected—one never knew what went together, and seemingly random acts could be cosmically related. Or perhaps the gnash of her teeth had backfired into her brain producing a surge of perceptivity, because Sukie now awed herself with a deduction: Nothing happens if you want it to.

He is gone. Believe it.

If you can believe it, he will turn up again.

Nothing happens if you want it to.

She wrote the lines in red. It was practically a poem. How cheering was that?

She ripped the page from her journal, went into the bathroom, taped the near-poem to the wall next to her beautiful mirror, and quickly memorized it.

"Hi, friend," she said to her reflection, playing Bobo, puffing herself up with a sharp intake of breath, letting her head loll forward and her shoulders hunch ever so slightly, achieving his arrogance and slouch all at once. "Hi, there," she growled, but then, with a saucy toss of her head, she switched over to being Sukie, not giving the time of day to the SOB (an expression her dad was fond of using for people he didn't like). She strutted, catching quick shots of herself at every angle as she moved in and out of reflection. "I'm in a restaurant—emerald-green walls, matching velvet upholstery, lit with a thousand candles so I'm bathed in the world's softest flickering amber, perhaps my hair appears so coppery and shimmering that the light dances off it." Was that possible? She wasn't sure, but she was tripping on the notion. Sukie's senses were so aroused, the fantasy so real, that in the mirror she saw herself through gossamer ribbons of smoke drifting upward. She felt the hushed curiosity of all present as she haughtily snaked between tables past a booth where Bobo, huddled with his buddies, drank Diet Coke and munched fries, unlike all the other diners, who sipped red wine from chic glasses, ones Sukie had seen at Restaurant Danielle in New York City on the occasion of her parents' anniversary. Those delicate crystal glasses, which people cradled, holding them gently underneath as if supporting a fragile blossom, were the essence of elegance. Bobo didn't have a clue, sitting there swigging soda out of an aluminum can. With a superior tilt of her chin, Sukie ignored the star quarterback, believing she was the first young woman in history to do so. To emphasize her disdain and to glory in it, she threw a backward glance over her shoulder into the mirror and saw her butt as wide as the back of an ox. It expanded further, stretching from one side of the mirror to the other. It was practically a planet. Sukie screamed.

Her father took the stairs two at a time. Mikey scrambled up behind him. He charged into her bedroom, halted—confused—then spied her in the bathroom. "What happened, baby? What's wrong?"

Sukie stood there woodenly.

"Sukie, talk to me." Her dad snapped his fingers, and she blinked, offering no explanation except to nudge him aside. He was blocking her view.

In the reflection, her backside now appeared neat, round, and tightly packaged in jeans, waist size 27. In other words, its normal self. Nothing like the twenty-pound ham hocks she'd witnessed a minute before. Nothing like Mars, or even a moon of Mars. Her dad tracked her gaze into the mirror, where he saw nothing unusual, then surveyed the room for clues to her behavior: the stubby vanilla-scented candles; her crowd of moisturizers, balms, and bath oils arranged around the edge of the tub by height as if someone were taking their class picture; the fluffy lavender bath towels folded and hung, with hand towels, also folded, centered over them. Sukie took pride in the presentation of her towels.

"Is this mirror, like, distorted?" asked Sukie.

"What are you talking about?"

"Is it a trick mirror, like in a fun house?"

"Don't be ridiculous. It's your grandmother's mirror. It's an antique."

Sukie continued to view with suspicion the slim reflection of her backside.

"Boy, it's smelly here." Mikey held his nose.

Her father blew out the candles. "Why did you scream, Sukie? You scared the hell out of me. I want an explanation."

My butt grew. It spread like batter on a griddle. Before my eyes. She thought that but didn't say it. Instead she waited for the mirror to play its tricks again.

Señor, lying on the floor with his legs splayed out, his tummy resting on the cool tiles, took no notice. Her dad contemplated the dog's lack of interest. "If Señor's not concerned, I guess I'm not either." He started out and stopped. "Don't ever scare me like that again."

"I won't, Daddy." Sukie used her squeakiest voice. She stuck her tongue out at him too, knowing he would find that simply adorable.

Dad

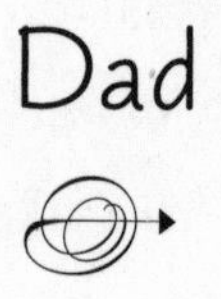

SHE aimed at Vince's chest, smacking the ball as hard as she could. He hopped sideways and popped it short, just over the net. Sukie sprinted. Grasping her racket in both hands, she slammed a backhand winner past him down the line.

"Time to stop, and that's a great shot to stop on," he called.

Sukie clamped her racket between her legs to have both hands free to refasten her hair in a clip. Her shirt stuck to her chest. She pulled it out and flapped it, wafting in cool air from the October day, then she swung the racket around and around, whipping it through the air. Sweat glistened on her forehead and dripped down her neck. She reveled in being utterly spent. Wearing herself out playing tennis brought her a sense of calm that nothing else did.

"Am I a killer?" she asked Vince as they picked up the balls. Sukie had a special way of collecting them. She lightly bopped a ball twice with her racket, it bounced up, and she caught it. To make a ball pop up off the ground took technique, and that as much as anything made her feel like a master of tennis. "Am I?"

"Potentially," said Vince. "But you've got some work to do deep down."

Boring. She didn't dare say that out loud, but deep down that is exactly what she thought. She walked over to fetch a ball that had landed way in the corner. When she turned around, Vince was toe-to-toe.

He poked a finger into her forehead. "There's marshmallow in there. But I like that you fired that ball straight at me. That's a good sign."

"Dad," she said. "His idea."

She could see him playing three courts over. He was easy to spot because he was tall and always wore an elasticized white terry band around his head. Sukie had tried to wear one once but it gave her a headache. Because he was in the middle of a point, she didn't wave. Sometimes she lifted her racket, signaling him, "Hey,

I'm here," a holdover from when she was little and her dad regularly took her to the amusement park. Every time she came around on the carousel, she waved and he waved back, and the carousel kept turning, carrying her again into the unknown and again back to Daddy.

Sukie loved the tennis club. There were precision-cut square hedges between courts and freshly mowed grass all around. When Sukie arrived for her private lesson at ten on Sunday morning, she always saw the mow marks. Sukie loved any way that anything could be made to look more orderly, including nature. She didn't like the ocean, a poetic deficiency she would rather die than admit. A walk on the beach gave her a severe case of the jumps. Those tumbling waves rushing toward her, the endless water, God knows what underneath.

If only the ocean could be mowed.

While she zipped her racket into a canvas bag and pulled on a sweatshirt, Vince gave her a pep talk. Sukie suppressed the inclination she had at every lesson to recommend sunblock, SPF 60. It was late for that anyway. From playing in the sun for years—Sukie guessed he was ancient, practically sixty—Vince's face was a leathery brown and creased in every direction. Even fine lines around his eyes and across his entire forehead crisscrossed, fascinating her. How did that happen?

"Who are you playing next week?" Vince scratched his potbelly.

"Copley Hills. They're tough."

"Picture yourself winning. That's the ticket. Visualize. Are you paying attention, missy? Look me in the eye."

Sukie focused.

"Do you see your opponent crumbling as your shots whiz by? Are you walking around with your arms aloft holding a trophy? Is the crowd cheering? Tell me."

"I'm holding a trophy." What an embarrassing thing to say.

"Eh, what?" Vince cocked an ear forward.

"I'm holding a trophy," she declared more boldly, still feeling idiotic.

He opened a cooler, handed her a water, and unscrewed one for himself. He took loud gulps. Sukie quenched her own sizable thirst silently, taking little sips, lots of them. She didn't like it when her body made noise.

Vince snapped the cap between his fingers. It flew through the air into the garbage can. "It won't happen unless you believe it."

Sukie choked. Some water came out of her nose. "What?"

"It won't happen unless you believe it. Nothing ever does."

"Is that true?"

"Ace true. Repeat that."

"Repeat what?" She pretended not to know because she didn't want to say it.

"Nothing happens unless you believe it."

"Nothing happens unless you believe it," she said.

"Like you mean it."

"Nothing happens unless you believe it." She verbally committed but quaked inside. What a nightmare. Wasn't that in conflict with "Nothing happens if you want it to," the truth Sukie had unearthed, the one that provided psychic comfort or potentially could if only she had mastered the not wanting part? Could love and tennis be polar opposites? Did you have to want it to win a game, but not want it to win love? Her brain clouded up. She was getting mixed up about which was which. Nothing happens if you want it to. Nothing happens unless you believe it. Suddenly they sounded the same but they weren't. How could she keep them straight? Should she do one and not the other? Which one?

Getting confused, Sukie instinctively reached for her phone, her security blanket. She snapped a picture of Vince, then of herself. She'd found that if she took a photo of the person she was with, the person never found it odd that she'd snapped a selfie as well. "Are you keeping a photographic record of our classes?" asked Vince.

"I may."

"Shoot, I left my hair at home."

Vince cracked that joke a lot. It must be hard to be bald, thought Sukie.

As soon as he greeted his next client, she deleted the photo of Vince and checked her selfie. She zoomed in on her mouth. Beads of sweat are sexy, she decided, admiring herself. Sweat was sexy if it didn't smell and was sprinkled as opposed to saturated (i.e. damp circles under the arms). Sukie never smelled because she was virtually laminated. Every morning and after every shower, she started in the middle of her arm, rolled the deodorant up to her armpit and then down her side halfway to her waist. In the sweat sense she was smell proof, but she was pleased to see delicate pearls of perspiration and a flattering pink in her cheeks.

Shouldering her heavy bag, she headed over to her dad. His match was over. Sukie was sure he'd won, he usually did, and he was chatting at the net with Frank, the man he always played with. Frank, divorced, was dating the club bartender, Marie, who always gave Sukie and Mikey free Cokes and as many pretzel sticks as they wanted. She frequently leaned across the bar to kiss Frank, and everyone turned to look. It drove Frank crazy. "Cut it out," he always said. "You'll get me thrown out."

"I flashed him once," she told Sukie and Mikey.

"What's that?" said Mikey.

"My boob. I flashed my naked boob at him. It was Sunday morning and all these uptight people were drinking Bloody Marys, and none of them noticed."

Mikey had fallen in love right then and there.

Whenever they came to the club, he snuck into the bar to see Marie, which wasn't allowed unless you were with a parent. Sukie always found him perched on a bar stool, waiting to see that boob, praying that she would flash it once more. No one had any idea of the fantastic amount of time Mikey spent thinking about Marie's boobs, or in what improbable context they figured.

The other night he'd built his mashed potatoes in the shape of a boob, Marie's, before he ate them.

Sukie suspected Mikey was hanging with Marie right now.

Her phone vibrated. She stopped. She had a text. Had she had it a minute ago and not even noticed? She tapped. It was from her mom. HOME BY THREE. DON'T BE SHOCKED. XOX MOM. Shocked? Why would she be shocked? Had her mom dropped a ton of weight at the spa? Did Dad know she was coming home today? "Hey, Dad!" Sukie clapped her hand over her mouth. What was she thinking? No one ever shouted near the courts. It could startle a player into missing a shot. She hurried instead while the phone vibrated again. She glanced down. Bobo.

Sukie slowed as a sense of gratitude suffused her, gratitude to whom she didn't know, but it was the most peaceful feeling. Probably the thanks were to herself for believing or not believing, or wanting or not wanting, or getting into whatever mind-set necessary to make this happen.

She was in no rush to read what he'd texted. She knew it could set off fireworks of anxiety or confusion.

Letting her duffel bag slide off her shoulder, she savored the moment, drinking in the letters identifying the texter, B-o-b-o.

That was her state of mind, looking inward with joy, not outward. It was a glorious autumn day. The leaf colors, vibrant oranges and yellows, might have been selected by Sukie's mom after studying swatches for months, the sky picked for its intense high-contrast cobalt blue. The outdoors mixed and matched, each element popped. "I could sell this day," her dad sometimes remarked when it was especially nice out, and, no question, today he could sell fall. And that is why it was even more remarkable that Sukie looked straight ahead and saw nothing but the happiness in her heart, and certainly not the man in the red Windbreaker who walked onto her dad's court. She didn't notice him until he punched her dad in the stomach and, when her dad doubled over, slugged him in the face. Her dad toppled as if he weighed nothing at all, the way Mikey's toy soldiers did when her brother once got into a rage and kicked them.

Flopman

"DADDY!"

Sukie streaked down the path, jumped a hedge, shortcut across the grass and jumped another hedge, and when she landed again on the brick path next to his court, crashed into a stroller. A drum beat in her chest—Be all right, be all right, be all right. "Daddy!" While her first bellow had been from shock, this second was a wail of worry. Warren Jamieson still lay flat. His tennis partner hunched over him. "Daddy," she called, "I'm coming, Daddy." Fear sucked her energy away in a sudden whoosh, and her legs weakened. Slogging along, her legs now as soft and heavy as sandbags, she let out great honking breaths that would have embarrassed her to death had she been remotely aware of them. She rubbed her hand across her face, her eyes were blurred. The man in the red Windbreaker strode toward her quickly.

Sukie shuddered backward, cowering, barely daring to blink. He passed, thank God, he passed. She had taken another heavy step forward when she felt her arm seized. Later she couldn't remember his face, just a grimness, and when he spoke he barely unclenched his jaw. "Your dad's slime. Never forget it."

Sukie yanked her arm free or thought she did. He might have released it. He kept going. Sukie swung around. Her dad was sitting up now.

Flopman.

He looked like Flopman, the stuffed body made from white sheets and string that their neighbors at their old house propped up on their porch each Halloween, next to a big pumpkin.

Frank, helping to position a towel on her father's bloody face, tilted her dad's head so his neck no longer appeared broken.

She ran onto the court. "Dad?" She squatted next to him.

He moved the towel so he could see her with half an eye. "Hey, kiddo."

She burst into uncontrollable tears, lost her balance, and plopped sideways.

"Stop, honey, baby, Daddy's okay."

Sukie, her ass on the asphalt, her legs splayed in front of her, let the tears fall.

A few club members were venturing hesitantly onto the court. They bent forward in a curious way as if they were looking for something suspicious under a house. Closing in, they lobbed inquiries: Was he all right, what happened? "Heart attack?" someone whispered, and someone else shook his head vigorously no.

"Call the police," Sukie blurted loudly.

The police. Bystanders spread that like gossip. A few produced phones.

"No, no." Her dad tried a laugh. "I think my daughter means I might need an ambulance, which I don't."

Sukie hadn't meant that at all. An ambulance? It hadn't crossed her mind, although perhaps it should have. What about the grim man in the red Windbreaker?

"Baby, get this damned headband off me."

Sukie scrambled up. She had a job with a grave responsibility. It was just like in those English movies on PBS where fashionable girls volunteered to become nurses, tending injured soldiers in World War II (or was it World War I, she was never sure), tenderly unwrapping bandages over hideous gaping wounds, their hair stylishly coiffed, their aprons stiff and spanking white with attractive red crosses on them. Now, with her dad able to speak, even summon his reassuring mellow confidence, she slipped into that familiar place where she wasn't only in the world—the world was watching.

She stood over her dad and, placing her hands on either side of his head, tugged gently. The band slipped up and off. She released the bloody side and held it gingerly by the clean side, pinching it between her fingers.

"Get Mikey," he instructed her. "Come on, Frank, help me up."

Frank locked his arm under her dad's. "One, two . . ." On Frank's "three," her dad made it to standing, although bent at the waist. Sukie could see that each breath he took hurt. "You might have a cracked rib," said Frank.

Sukie remained mesmerized by her dad's painful breathing.

"Get your brother," he told her. "Hurry up. Meet me at the car."

With all eyes on her, inflating the importance of her mission, Sukie flew to do her father's bidding. She couldn't help but notice as she ran swiftly that players on every court had stopped their games. At the net, on the baseline, wherever the last point had left them, they stayed. Alerted initially by Sukie's shriek, they had halted their own dramas to make sense of her dad's.

Sukie tore into the clubhouse and stopped at the entrance to the bar. "Mikey." She waved him toward her. When he casually spun on the bar stool, a row of pretzel sticks poking out of his mouth, she marched over and roughly yanked him. "Hurry up."

"Ow." He jerked his arm away.

"Someone hurt Dad. Just shut up and come."

Mikey, racing to keep up as they rushed to the car, kept asking what happened, and Sukie refused to tell him, partly to keep him agitated, he deserved it, though she wasn't sure why, and partly because she was so anxious herself.

Mom

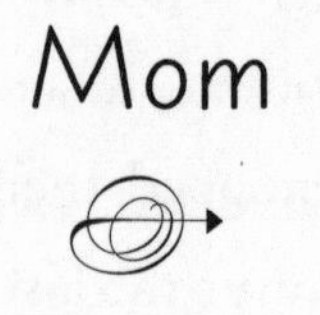

"I GOT into a fistfight," her dad told Mikey, who fell silent at the sight of him and behaved, in Sukie's opinion, in a way that no one should.

"Stop staring." She slapped Mikey on the back, although she was just as riveted as he was by the sight of her agile dad, bent and bloodied, moving across the gravel as if every step were an accomplishment.

When the whole family had first visited their nearly finished, brand-new development home, it was sitting on a dirt lot on Lilac Drive, bare except for four birch trees. Their tall skinny trunks had twiggy branches lush with leaves. "Don't love them, they're history," her dad told her mom. "They're growing where the driveway's going." A man was already sawing one of them, and it was tilting, tilting, tilting. Then it fell, not with a crash but with a slow sigh. Sukie kept imagining that her dad would sigh over in the same way, but he didn't. With Frank's help, he wedged his body behind the wheel. Not easy. The strain and pain were biological proof of how everything is connected: His stomach hurt, and his muscles and ribs were bruised, which meant that to get his legs into the car, he had to lift each one up and into driving position. Every so often his lips tightened into a wince, causing his eyes to squint and then fly wide open when the squinting triggered pain in his cheek, where a red bruise spread from there down the left side of his face.

"Get in back, hurry up, dope." She pushed Mikey in.

"Who'd you fight with?" Mikey asked as they drove home.

"An idiot."

"Why?"

"Business. It's just business."

"What business?"

"Leave Dad alone. He's hurt," said Sukie.

"A building," said her dad. "He wants it, I got it. He's a sore loser."

"Are you in the mob?" asked Mikey.

"Nothing as interesting as that."

"Mom's coming home today," Sukie piped up, realizing as she said it how happy and relieved she was. "She said she'd be home by three. She texted me—" Sukie did not fully get the word "me" out of her mouth. It died on her lips, dealt a knockout blow by the word "texted," which she said, and then heard, and then remembered.

Her breath caught in her chest. With sharp, shrieking intakes she fought for air.

"What the hell?" Her dad braked quickly.

Her elbows winged up, a spasm. Was she going to flap like her mom? Am I a flapper? Is it genetic? Strange thoughts can flit through your head even when you're struggling to do something as essential as breathing. Perhaps if she'd leaped off a skyscraper, she might think, My hair's dirty, or I wish I had a cat, before she hit the sidewalk. Or, as a noose tightened around her neck, which was exactly how Sukie felt this second, she might be struck with one last burst of self-knowledge: I'm a flapper too.

"Get air," her dad barked.

She hit the button to lower the window.

"Put your head down," he said, and unsnapped her seat belt.

She bent forward and let her head drop between her knees. "My cell," she choked out.

"Yourself?"

"My cell. My cell phone. It's gone!" Her wail broke the jam—she could breathe again.

"Are you kidding?"

She sat up. "No."

"You mean this fit is about your phone? Your silly phone?"

"I must have dropped it. When I was running. When I saw you. My racket, too." Her bottom lip trembled.

"Christ." Her dad smacked the steering wheel. "Are you going to cry?"

Sukie shook her head.

He shot Mikey a look in the rearview mirror. "What about you?"

Mikey shrank back in his seat.

Her dad reached to open the glove compartment but gave up with a grimace. "Christ," he said again, and there was blame in his voice. Sukie could hear it. It was her fault for making him forget his injuries and do something as stupid as reach. "My phone's in the glove compartment. Call a friend at the club and ask her to find it."

"Can we go back?"

"No."

"My whole life is in that phone," said Sukie. But what she was thinking was, My heart is in that phone. Maybe my future. Bobo's text. She'd never get to read it.

"I'm not going back to the club." Her dad pulled into traffic.

He's never going back to the club. How did she know that? Why did she know that?

"Don't you have a friend at the club?"

"No," said Sukie.

"No one?" He threw her a curious look.

"No." She kept her eyes low.

"Then call Mrs. Merenda and ask her to look for your stuff. I'm sure someone found it."

Sukie took her dad's phone out of the glove compartment. She punched in her own number. Answer, someone please answer, she prayed, and then reversed herself, Don't answer, please don't answer. Was it better if someone had her precious cell phone with Bobo's text message in it, or was it better if the phone was lying on the grass somewhere waiting to be found? After a bunch of rings she heard her own voice, "Hi, this is Sukie, I really appreciate your call. Leave a message please." *Oh, man, could my voice-mail message be any more lame?* Sukie clicked off with dismay and dialed the club.

"Hi, Mrs. Merenda," Sukie chirped so adorably, so innocently, so helplessly that she might be a baby chick who had broken its shell and was announcing its arrival to the world. She laid her catastrophe on Mrs. Merenda in an endless run-on sentence, the words tumbling after one another, some um's and uh's sprinkled in to generate maximum sympathy.

"I'm sorry," said Mrs. Merenda. "Someone was talking to me, could you repeat that?"

Sukie flatly supplied the facts. "I dropped my cell phone and duffel bag somewhere between courts three and five when my father—"

"Yes," said Mrs. Merenda.

The "yes" threw her. She sensed disapproval. What had she done wrong? Or was it her father? Did Mrs. Merenda think her dad was slime?

"Do you have it, by any chance?" said Sukie. "Did anyone turn it in?"

"No."

"Will you look?"

"Yes."

"When?"

But there was a click. Sukie put the phone back in the glove compartment.

From Bobo. She saw the words suspended in space. Like skywriting, they diffused and slowly evaporated, leaving a smudge and then nothing, no proof that they were ever there to begin with.

"I'm sure she'll find it," said her dad.

"Maybe I'll find it in the mirror."

"What's that supposed to mean?"

"I don't know."

They turned down Lilac Drive. Sukie, depressed, didn't immediately notice the black car in front of their house. A hat emerged—a lady's straw hat with a wide curved brim and a trim of black ribbon. The wind caught it, flapping the brim, and a woman's hand clamped it down. At the same time, the trunk popped open and inside Sukie saw pink. The woman in the hat had to be her mother, because her mother had luggage the color of bubble gum.

The driver took out her mother's bag and carried it to the door.

Sukie yelled out the window, "Mom!"

Her mother, still holding her hat in place, whirled around to wave. She wore sunglasses—large ones with black frames, the kind movie stars wore when they didn't want to be seen and wanted to attract attention all at the same time—and she had a long scarf wound around her neck a million times with still enough length to trail in a divinely nonchalant way. Sometimes to see your mom from afar is to see a different person. The woman other people see when they look. My mom is a stunner, thought Sukie. The most stylish ever. I bet Dad thinks so too. I bet when he met this glamorous woman, he was swept away.

Her dad stopped the car so Sukie and Mikey could greet their mom before he pulled into the driveway. Normally Mikey raced while Sukie sauntered, her butt a slow swinging pendulum, a move she'd perfected. Today, overwhelmed, relieved, she bolted across the grass, her arms out. "Mom!"

Her mom shied backward. "No, no, no."

Sukie and Mikey, speeding toward her, stopped in time.

"No hugs. Just air kisses for now." Her mom puckered and sent them three, "*P-P-P.*"

"Oh, my God!" Sukie's hands flew to her heart. "Mom, what happened, were you in an accident?"

Not visible from afar, close up an astonishment: Her mom's nose was bandaged, taped down and across, bits of gauze peeking out underneath, a snow-covered mountain in the middle of her face.

The Faraway Truth and the Truth Close Up

"WERE you in a fight too?" asked Mikey.

Her mother started to laugh, at least that's what Sukie thought. It was hard to tell because not much of her mom was visible between the glasses, the bandage, and the rest of the getup, but her lips did widen, a giggle might have erupted before she stiffened. "Don't make me smile," she said. "It's dangerous."

"How come?" said Mikey.

"What happened to your nose?" asked Sukie.

"I have to go to bed, I'm not myself yet. Oops, what is that? I thought I saw a wolf. Hi, Señor." Her mother rapped the glass pane next to the door. Through it Señor, inside, watched them. "What a day, isn't it beautiful? It's hard to talk, it is." She pressed her hand against her lips. "I'm sewn together." She started to smile again and again stiffened. "Who got into a fight?"

The car door slammed. They all turned to watch Sukie's dad ache his way over.

"Warren? Warren, what happened?"

"Do you want to see the buffalo nickel that Marie gave me?" Mikey pulled it from his pocket.

"Hold it up, I can't look down."

"Why not?"

"Mom, what's wrong with your nose?" Sukie, loud now and insistent, still got no reply, because her mom was quizzing her dad about why he could barely walk and had a bruise bulging like a plum on the side of his face, and her dad was refusing to answer except with one word, "Later."

"Peas, you need peas. *You* need peas, not me. Isn't it great that I told you to buy peas? Did you remember to get the peas?" said Sukie's mom.

Her dad nodded.

"I must have known somehow that someone would need them. Ouch. Don't make me talk. This is so thoughtless, Warren, I can't make that many expressions yet."

"Mom, tell me," Sukie begged.

Her mom thrust her purse into Sukie's arms. "Open the door for me, would you? I can't look for my keys, it's dangerous."

"That's dangerous too?" said Mikey.

"Oh, for God's sake, Felice," said her dad.

"You think I'm exaggerating. If you'd visited me, you'd know. I'm not supposed to look down." Her mom took off her dark glasses, breaking the news. Her face appeared to have swallowed her eyes, because the flesh was so swollen and bruised black and blue that her mom's eyes were reduced to peepholes. "I don't mean to shock you," she told her kids, "but your father forced me."

Mikey started to cry.

"Calm down," her dad said. "Your mom got a facelift. That's all." He opened the door. "It's no big deal."

"But your nose," said Sukie.

"It was driving me crazy," said her mom. "And if you'd suffered the way I had, you'd think it was a big deal. Take my bag upstairs, would you, Sukie? Obviously your father's useless."

Sukie rolled it into the house. "What about your

nose was driving you crazy?" She and her mom had the same nose. They both had little ramps from top to tip. They were both—Sukie recalled that website—"ramp."

"Ramp?" said Sukie. "Was that what drove you crazy?"

"Ramp? What are you talking about?"

"How was the spa?" asked Mikey, wiping his eyes.

Sukie dragged the heavy suitcase from step to step. "She wasn't at the spa, Mikey. Come on. I'll explain later."

He ran up the stairs, happy to be with his sister.

In the Jamiesons' showcase of a house, the large foyer with a marble floor soared two stories. The staircase, a winding affair, had a lacquered wood banister with white balusters that wrapped the open upstairs hall. Sukie, wheeling her mom's suitcase, stopped to look down at her parents. Mikey bumped into her and stayed there. She put her arm around him. Again from a distance, with the brim of the hat obscuring her mother's face, the winding scarf concealing God knows how many stitches, Sukie was once again struck by her mother's chic and how different things can seem from far away, how there's more than one truth, the faraway truth and the truth close up.

"I can't deal with this now," her mom was saying.

"There's nothing to deal with," said her dad.

Their voices were low but traveled easily. Sukie and Mikey didn't have to strain to hear.

"I can't believe you did this."

"What?" said her dad.

"This is my day."

"Your day?"

"My homecoming. I need care."

A red rubber ball fell between the balusters. Sukie, watching her parents, didn't see the small ball until, on its way down, it entered her sight range and hit the marble floor.

Hearing the thump, her parents turned to see Señor's ball rolling toward them. "Oh my God, I looked down," her mother shrieked. Sukie pulled Mikey back just as her parents gazed upward to see where it had come from. Her mother's hand flew to her neck with another shriek. "I'm not supposed to look up, either."

Señor's fur brushed Sukie's legs. Even though the

dog moved through the hall at his own deliberate pace, by the time Sukie realized the tickle was Señor, all she saw was his rump and the curl of a tail disappearing into her room.

The Text

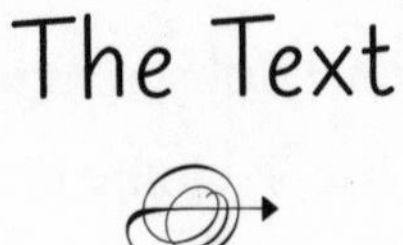

"BUT Mom, we have the same nose."

"Not anymore," said her mom cheerfully, now ensconced on the bed, surrounded by mail, slicing open some envelopes with her nail file but tossing most into a junk pile. "Where's Señor? Why isn't Señor here? Señor?" she called. "He's rejecting me, what can I do? How have you been? Tell me everything." Her mom patted the bed for Sukie to sit.

"How did you change it?" asked Sukie, standing in the doorway. She'd been twirling her hair nervously and was surprised to discover that she'd yanked out some strands.

"Well, aren't you a broken record. It's just one piece of the pie."

"What pie?" Sukie didn't know what to do with the hair in her hand. She stuck it in her pocket.

"My face. Stop obsessing."

"I'm not obsessing."

"You are obviously obsessing. I obsess, so don't tell me you don't obsess. Come on, sit, talk."

"Today was horrible," said Sukie.

Her mother flinched. "Don't touch your stitches," she scolded herself. She slapped her own hand, which had misbehaved and scratched a spot under her ear. "My whole scalp itches," she confided. "I have a staple in my head. What happened?"

"My phone. I lost it. At the club."

"They'll find it, I'm sure. Don't go getting hysterical."

"I'm not hysterical," said Sukie, wondering if she was.

"Because you're always getting hysterical."

"No, I'm not."

"Don't bother to deny it. Doesn't Sukie get hysterical?" she asked her husband, who had creaked in carrying a bag of frozen peas. He carefully lowered himself into an armchair, flicked on the TV, and pressed the bag against the bruised and battered side of his face. "Doesn't she?"

Sukie's dad simply winked at Sukie with his only visible eye.

Her mom perused a letter. "Well, this is inconvenient."

"What?" said Sukie.

"The big school meeting about college is Wednesday night."

"You don't have to go," said Sukie.

"Of course we have to go."

"This counts, kiddo. Big time," said her dad.

"No, really, you don't have to go."

How would she explain her mother? What lie would cover it? A box fell on her head. A spa accident. What was a spa accident? Sukie's mind was racing while her mother prattled on. "You have to get into the best college. We have to make sure that we're doing everything and that you're doing everything. Perhaps you should volunteer at a homeless shelter. Is there one nearby? That would be so wonderful for your college application. We'll see what they say on Wednesday. We're not the kind of parents who don't care that we're not doing everything possible for your future. Look at me, Susannah Danielle Jamieson."

Sukie twisted to face her mom directly, realizing as she did so that her mom had pieces of Scotch tape next to her eyes and below her ears.

"We love you," said her mom.

"I love you, too," said Sukie. "What's that tape for?"

"To hold my stitches in place." Her mom leaned close. Sukie could see the bits of black thread underneath.

"How long does the tape stay there?"

"Until the stitches come out. Listen, darling, don't worry. I'll wrap myself in something fantastic. No one will ever know."

Sukie wandered out of her parents' bedroom and into her own. Señor was waiting. She looked into his eyes. She often did that to channel his strength, his confidence, his judgment, or another of his gifts that she wished she possessed. Today, feeling the damp sweat that heralded the onset of the jumps, she searched for Señor's stillness, hoping to shore up her own. After a minute of silence, Señor made himself clear. "I know," said Sukie, "but who?" She didn't have a close friend. She liked Jenna, but Jenna was best friends with Frannie. Sukie couldn't possibly spend time with Frannie. She couldn't even look her in the eye.

Maybe Issy would understand. She was older, but she was so friendly and warm. Still, Sukie couldn't just turn up at Clementi's, order a pizza, and pour out her heart.

A true friend. She was reluctant to write how much she longed for one even in her private journal, for her eyes only.

Usually she pushed it out of her head.

She planned her school days judiciously, making sure she had a meeting every lunch—Educating Girls Globally, Debate Club, Spanish Club, Math Club. On Fridays, when there were no meetings, she went to the cafeteria. Kids never minded if she joined their table, but no one ever called her over or saved her a seat. Sometimes she sat alone, spread papers around as if she needed the entire space, and knocked off the weekend's homework. By these means, if she didn't stop herself from feeling lonely, she at least kept everyone else from thinking that she was. Friendless. The bleak word skittered around the fringes of her mind, scurried ahead of her through the halls, clearing the empty way.

In her journal she railed against the unfairness of it. *It's not my fault that I'm the total package, looks and brains. Everyone's jealous.* That, she told herself, was why her cell phone hardly rang, even though every week she changed the ring as if the ring tone had become stuck in her head from hearing it again and again and again.

Bobo.

She let herself fall backward onto the bed and crossed her arms over her face. This was a way not to cry. Tried and true. Tears could trickle out, but mostly, in this position, her eyes would simply fill to the brim like glasses of water.

Your dad's slime.

Already she could hardly remember the grim man's face, only his red Windbreaker and his thin lips barely moving. He hadn't spoken in a threatening way, more as if he were breaking the news, tipping her to it.

Your dad's slime. Never forget it.

Bury it. Bury it deep. It's not a truth, it's a falsehood. A horrible lie. Blot it out. Think about something else—ice cream, dancing elephants, Señor's eyes. Bobo. Think about Bobo. *Your dad's slime. Never forget it.* She had buried it and already it rose from the grave.

Sit up. That's an order.

It wasn't Señor's idea, it was Sukie's, but she knew he would approve.

She stormed into the bathroom and faced the mirror. "Don't feel sorry for yourself," she ordered. "Hup, two, three, four." Calling out the numbers, she marched in a circle until she came face-to-face with herself again, and then, almost as if someone were beckoning her, she drew closer.

"If I can't have an actual friend, I want a friend in the mirror," Sukie announced, and, in a blink, instead of her own reflection she beheld Issy with her punky pink hair and sly eyes twinkling with fun. Issy was wearing an outfit Sukie had once admired—a baby-doll dress with straps that came over her shoulders, crisscrossed under her breasts, and wound around her body at least two more times (binding her tiny waist snugly) with still enough length for her to twirl the ends languidly as Issy in the mirror was doing right now. It was a summer dress, but Isabella, who Sukie suspected never did the obvious, wore it in cold weather as a jumper with a long-sleeved jersey underneath. "I love your dress," said Sukie.

"You can borrow it," said Issy. "Anytime. We should go shopping."

"I'd love that," said Sukie.

Issy smiled her wonderful, wide, and welcoming smile. "If I had a little sister, I'd want her to be you."

"Thank you," said Sukie. "Today, especially, I really need that."

Issy disappeared from the mirror, and the good feeling generated by an imaginary visit with Issy dissolved as Sukie confronted her own nose.

From the tip to the top, she pinched it, trying to round the narrow flat ramp.

Scotch tape. That's what she needed.

Sukie had a label maker. She used it to identify things that didn't need identifying, like her Scotch-tape dispenser. She'd printed SUKIE'S SCOTCH TAPE and stuck it on. The label wasn't a warning to her younger brother: "This is mine, don't touch." She just loved to label. Everything that could be labeled was labeled, and had assigned seating across the top of her desk. A place for everything, everything in its place. In rows straight and even. The Jamiesons' housekeeper, Louisa, who came in twice a week, marveled at

Sukie's order and at how little work she had to do in Sukie's compulsively arranged room. Lopsided equals bad luck, Sukie believed it utterly. She tore off short strips of tape, about two inches, sticking one on each fingertip. If she fluttered her fingers, they waved like flags.

Returning to the mirror, she stripped the tape bits off and, so that they would be handy when she needed them, stuck them on the silver frame. As she did, she leaned sideways. She could still look at herself, but at the same time she could see back through the doorway into her bedroom where the telephone sat. "Do it." She cracked the whip. "Just do it. Grow up, you miserable baby."

She marched to the desk and dialed.

The phone rang and rang. To distract herself from the depressingly inevitable—no answer—she examined her cuticles.

"Shoot, how does this work?"

"I can hear you," yelped Sukie.

"Who is this?" The man sounded amused.

"Susannah Jamieson. This is my cell. You have my cell."

"Warren's kid?"

Sukie tried to tell if he disapproved of her dad, but it wasn't like talking to Mrs. Merenda, where she sensed something weird. "Yes," she said. "I dropped it at the club."

"Here you go."

"What?"

"I was talking to the conductor."

"The conductor?"

"I'm on the train."

"The train?"

"I'll have some of those, please. Sorry. Wait a second while I pay for this."

Sukie straightened the stapler. She turned the mug of pens so SUKIE'S SHARPIES faced front. Lopsided equals bad luck. Lopsided equals bad luck.

"I'm sorry," said the man. "I meant to leave your phone at the club, but I put it in my pocket and forgot all about it until it just now rang. I'll cruise by your house and drop it off as soon as I get back."

She tapped down the paper clips so she could close the box neatly. "Back from where?" she asked.

"New York City."

Her phone was on its way to New York City. "When are you coming back?"

"Wednesday."

Four whole days. She wanted to bang her head against the wall. She really did. She wanted to walk over to the wall and knock herself out.

"You know what? I'll drop it at your dad's office. I'm Glen Harbinder. Your dad knows me."

Sukie adjusted the label maker. Now everything on her desk was straight. Later she wrote in her journal, *Emotionally I was at the edge of a cliff. Should I leap? I closed my eyes.*

Sukie leaped. "Would you please read me my text message?" She trotted out her most pitiful little-girl voice.

"How do I do that?" he asked.

"Touch the little green square at the top."

"Got it. You've got two."

"Two?" Sukie's eyes snapped open.

"Two from Bobo." He enjoyed the name, she could tell. She could hear him thinking, How cute.

"What's the capital of North Dakota?"

"That's the message?"

"No, I'm not telling you the message until you answer the question." He chuckled, or maybe chewed.

"Bismarck." God, was he mentally ill? She knew them all. She could recite the presidents backward and forward. Who did he think he was dealing with?

"'Meet me after the game.'"

"That's the message?"

"And the other is 'Danger cation.'"

"What?"

"'Danger cation.'"

"Is that one word?"

"No, two."

"Would you spell it?"

"D-A-N-G-E-R C-A-T-I-O-N."

She hung up and began jumping. She bounced into the bathroom and back into the bedroom. MEET ME AFTER THE GAME. DANGER CATION. Cation? Cation? Caution. He must mean caution!

MEET ME AFTER THE GAME. DANGER CAUTION.

Definitely caution. He must have misspelled it. Everyone makes mistakes texting. Lots of really smart people were bad spellers too. She'd heard that somewhere.

DANGER CAUTION.

He is not only a bad speller, he is bad. She'd never known a guy who was bad. There was no one bad at

Cobweb. Kids there were sickeningly decent. ROLL ME OVER. Sukie was tingling.

Thank God she'd straightened everything on her desk. Who cared that he couldn't spell? She was a good-enough speller for both of them. With luck, their children would take after her.

Facial Engineering

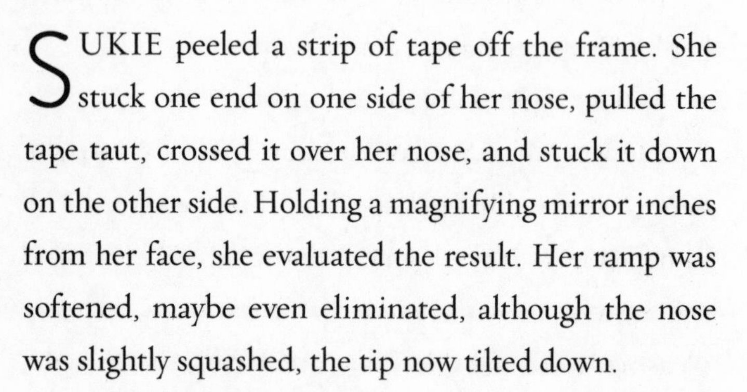

SUKIE peeled a strip of tape off the frame. She stuck one end on one side of her nose, pulled the tape taut, crossed it over her nose, and stuck it down on the other side. Holding a magnifying mirror inches from her face, she evaluated the result. Her ramp was softened, maybe even eliminated, although the nose was slightly squashed, the tip now tilted down.

She stuck the end of a second piece of tape to the tip of her nose and pulled—not too forcibly or it would detach from the tip, not too gently or it wouldn't correct the squash and the unattractive downward tilt. The procedure took patience and concentration. She might have been performing microsurgery.

She was excited, which made it hard to focus. How

quickly her anxieties about her dad and the grim man had flown from her head at the prospect of seeing Bobo. She'd Googled the Hudson Glen High School calendar of sports events. His game was next Saturday afternoon. She pulled the tape up vertically—the idea was to raise her nose tip and keep it anchored in a slightly elevated position. It was an ingenious piece of facial engineering, and she congratulated herself silently when she pressed the other end of the tape between her eyes and, as she released it and lowered her hands to her sides, it stayed stuck.

Señor caught Sukie's eye in the mirror.

He was right. She couldn't say, "You are so right, Señor." She couldn't risk speaking, but she agreed with him. Her nose did look snub. Almost "Miss Piggy." And the Scotch tape on her face distracted from her more pleasing features. I'd kill for candlelight, she thought, but she knew that striking a match might send a quiver through her body, causing all the tape to fall off her nose. She dimmed the overhead light to its lowest and softest glow.

Having done that, she moved slowly backward to the opposite wall, and there in the twilight of twenty watts, she gazed into the mirror at the faraway truth.

Her face was perfection.

If only she could stay eight feet away from Bobo, with a taped nose and in near darkness at all times.

"Bobo." She tried out his name, but her voice was flat, without allure.

She needed clothes to find her voice. The wrinkled tennis shorts and white tee she wore were worse than useless. They were an obstacle.

A party dress in silk charmeuse? Charmeuse. The word, vaguely foreign sounding, conjured up misty, clinging, sheer, something worn by a woman lost in a fog. Although recently in *Teen Vogue* she'd seen a fashion spread of puffy charmeuse dresses, some with gathered high waists that hid one's body as successfully as a tent. Those charmeuse dresses were girlish, too skipping-through-daisies.

Her mother had a black silk jersey tunic, and Sukie loved the cool, slinky feel of it. Once, when her mom was out, she'd tried it on and danced, enjoying that every bounce and tremble of her breasts was revealed and yet remained invisible. Sukie had a vague notion that showing and hiding at the same time was more enticing than just showing or just hiding. This was all because of Bobo. Meeting him had opened her up to a whole new way of thinking: What was hot and what wasn't? Silk jersey was sophisticated, too.

Fixing the mirror with a hypnotic stare, she saw herself dressed in a loose white silk jersey top with a V neckline. A deep V, she corrected, increasing the angle enough to reveal cleavage. Nice. Very nice. She needed a bottom—a black skirt as tight as a snake's skin, slit to her thigh, accessorized with a wide belt slung low on her hips.

Picturing this, she spoke his name. "Bobo." Her voice came out satisfyingly sultry.

Let the games continue.

"Hi, yes, fine, terrific." Words all murmured, well, imagined to be murmured as Bobo circled her, nuzzling her neck. She broke away and ran down the field until he tackled her.

No, start earlier. Much earlier. An unearthly sunset. In the mirror she envisioned it: The sun, an acid orange, scorched the horizon, and Sukie stood alone, framed by a fiery sky the way an angel has a halo or the Statue of Liberty a spiked crown. The heat of the sun burns inside me, she thought, thrilled that her skin might be so hot to the touch that Bobo, stealing a kiss, might have to run his lips under cold water or rub on vitamin E. In spiked heels she traversed the football field, scuffing up white dust from the lines of the touchdown zone. Ahead, swarms of people gathered at the entrance to the locker room. She sauntered up behind a phalanx of silly screaming girls. Over their shoulders Sukie could see one player after another drift out. They were tired, spent, but revved by the fans cheering their victory. Sukie ruffled her hair so the gentle waves framed and flattered. "I am tall enough that a man who aims to find me can find me," Mirror Sukie assured herself. Mirror Sukie didn't worry that the tape would fall off her nose. In the mirror, now, her nose appeared corrected, rampless, no tape necessary. The sunset shimmered in intense heat, and for an instant the words DANGER CAUTION blazed. Just then the star quarterback ambled out, his hair still wet from the shower, stuck down in clumps. Even if I hadn't seen him shake his head as adorably as a wet puppy, spraying drops in every direction, thought Sukie, I would know he was there from the chanting. "Go-bo Bobo, Go-bo Bobo, Go-bo Bobo." With his confident slouch and lazy smile, he soaked up the adulation. At the same time, he searched. No one could tell. In the football game he dodged, ducked, spun, and sprinted, but off the field Bobo was a study in minimalism.

His pupils flicked left to right. Giving no indication that the prize had been spotted, he eased forward slowly, and the cheering hordes pressed in. Ignoring them, he kept walking, and the fans, receiving neither encouragement nor resistance, no sense that they even existed, soon fell silent and drew back, providing a pathway straight to Sukie.

She slipped off her shoes and ran. Thank God for the slit in her skirt. Her running skills were on display. She too was an athlete.

They streaked down the field. She felt him closing in and slowed to provide the opportunity. He lunged and took her down, the deer slain by the hunter. They fell onto soft earth. "Roll me over," said Sukie, and he did.

"Your nose," he said.

"My nose?"

She sat up. In the mirror she saw the ramp spread, its edges sharpen. She had a road down her nose.

Sukie screamed.

Her mother screamed.

Señor screamed.

"Oh my God," her mom wailed. "You scared me. I came in to say good-night and you made me scream again."

Sukie jammed her face smack against the mirror. The taped construction had collapsed and her nose had returned to its normal ramped state. No longer a two-lane highway. No longer a runway for jet planes, or a football field where Bobo could be blitzing or being blitzed. Tape dangled half on, half off.

"What's that tape on your nose? Are you making fun of me?"

"No."

Her mother carried on piteously. "I've done nothing but scream since I've been home, and make faces I am absolutely not supposed to make. You and your father. And you know what? I'm not even allowed to cry." She pushed Sukie aside to see in the mirror what damage had been done. She felt her neck and around her eyes and then slapped her hand again for misbehaving.

"Oh my God." Sukie pointed to a tiny hairline crack. It meandered from one side of the mirror to the other about six inches from the bottom. She felt it. "The mirror just cracked. It cracked. How did it crack?"

"What did you do?"

"Nothing, I swear. I didn't do anything. How could I do that?" Sukie, who specialized in fake baby voices, didn't realize that she was squealing like a toddler.

Her mother raised the dimmer switch. In the unflattering overhead light, her mom's face, swollen and pulpy, had a startlingly varied color palette. It reminded Sukie of the streaky mess that results when kids mush their finger paints together. "This is why I couldn't live with my face," said her mom.

Sukie wasn't following. "Because of the mirror?"

"Decay."

"Decay? What are you talking about? You're only forty-one."

Her mother ran her finger along the hairline crack. "Eventually everything goes."

"Why did you change your nose?" asked Sukie.

"I hated it."

"You hated it? Hated?" Sukie sat with a thump on the side of the tub.

"For goodness' sakes, so what?"

Sukie stared at her feet. Her pinkie toe on her left foot was longer than her fourth toe. She'd forgotten that. Weren't toes supposed to get smaller from one to the other? "Did you touch Señor's feet?"

"Of course not."

"Then why did he scream? He only screams when people touch his feet." To trim his claws, the vet had to anesthetize him, because Señor uttered a yelp so shrill it could blow everyone's eardrums. "You touched his feet," said Sukie. "You did."

"Don't be ridiculous."

"Bitch," Sukie muttered. It was the first time in her life she'd called her mother a bitch, and she had no idea why she'd said it. It scared her a little.

"What did you say?"

"Nothing."

After a silence of mutual dislike they turned to Señor. What would he tell them, how might he scold them or provide some perspective? But he was having none of it. His jaw was set, his nostrils quivered, but Sukie and her mom rightly deduced that he had picked up the scent from the pizza delivery truck. They'd seen that look before.

"We had the same nose," said Sukie plaintively.

"Mine was more pointed than yours."

"No, it wasn't."

"Yes, right at the tip." Her mom ripped the tape off Sukie's face and left.

Sukie slumped. Her arms hung limply, her bare knees knocked together. In this deflated pose, didn't she look a little like a junkie? Didn't she? She peeked in the mirror. Maybe. Anyway that wasn't the point, she reminded herself. The point was, Her nose was awful. Her nose was so awful that her mother had it fixed. The point was, How can I take this nose to meet Bobo?

"Hey."

Sukie jerked up. "Dad?" She craned her head. He was in her bedroom. She got up slowly, exhausted, and joined him. "Are you in pain, Dad?"

"Nothing I can't handle." He grinned at her in a way that Sukie knew meant he had more to say. She waited while his smile bled off. He rubbed his fist against his lips. "Better not to talk about it," he said finally. "You know, out there."

She knew exactly what he meant, his incident on the tennis court. "Of course. I wouldn't."

He picked up *Madame Bovary* and examined the front cover, which pictured a woman with a lovely long arched neck, her eyes closed, her face suffused in either emotional pain or thrall. He turned it over and read the back. "An adulteress, huh?"

"It's really good. It was shocking when it was written."

"Good for you."

She didn't quite know what he meant by that.

He placed the book back on the desk, taking extra care to center it exactly the way Sukie had placed it originally. "I got a call from the hotel, the one where she stayed after her surgery. She took a duvet."

"What?"

"Yep. She just took it. Packed it up."

"Wow. How'd she squish it in? I mean into her suitcase?"

He pointed his finger at Sukie as if he had the answer and then let his hand slap down by his side. "Three hundred sixty dollars. I told them to put it on the credit card."

"Why did she take it?"

"When you figure that out, let me know." Sukie and her dad laughed. "Don't tell her I told you."

"I won't." Whatever her dad wanted, she would honor.

After a moment he said, "Promise?"

"I promise." She spoke up louder because he seemed lost in thought. "Did you like Mom's nose before she changed it?"

He shrugged.

Sukie pressed. "Did you hate her nose before? Did you think it was ugly?"

"Crazy, really." He might have been talking to himself, the way he said it, ever so quietly. Sukie waited for more, but he just rubbed his hand over his face. He walked over to her penguins and picked up Daphne, who had eyelashes and plaid wings. "Hey, I won this, didn't I? At Magic Mountain."

"Mom's going to that school meeting about college. I don't know what to tell kids."

"About what?" He turned around. "Her face?"

Sukie nodded.

"You'll think of something."

The Lie

SHE settled on a story and planted it in the locker room, the most fertile soil.

"What?" Fleur erupted. Fleur's "what" was more squawk than question. It rattled metal lockers, bounced off the cement walls, pierced the isolation of iPods, and spread the word: Something had happened.

"Thank God she's all right," said Sukie. She laced up her sneakers, keeping her head down, listening to the chorus of questions from the rest of third-period gym, and letting Fleur answer them.

"Her mom broke her nose."

"How did it happen?" asked Jenna.

"At the spa. She dove into the shallow end."

Denicia felt her own nose. It was still there in one

piece. It was impossible to hear about Sukie's mom and not recall her own carefree race to a pool on a summer's day and a headfirst plunge. She'd done it many times, hadn't they all? A headfirst plunge and a surprising smack. That part hadn't happened, but it could have.

"She could be paralyzed," said Autumn.

Autumn, who dreamed of becoming an actress, was admired for her bones. Her hips poked out like sticks. You could shelve books on her collarbones. No one had ever seen her throw up or even diet. Her metabolism appeared to be one of those truly unfair things in life. When she spoke the line "She could be paralyzed," her eyes widened as if she beheld her own mother bandaged like a mummy in a hospital bed. She was unbuttoning her blouse to change into the navy Cobweb gym shirt, and her hands fumbled, unable to complete the task. "Paralyzed." Once she said it, the word was picked up and repeated. What hadn't happened was more exciting than what had.

"She's not paralyzed," said Fleur. "Is she?"

"No, just her nose. It got . . ." Sukie flat-handed her own nose, indicating it was smashed.

"How frightening," said Frannie gravely.

Sukie, startled by the genuine concern and wishing

with all her heart that she hadn't lied, dug herself in deeper. "It was scary when we got the call. I saw in my dad's face that something horrible had happened."

Sukie did see her dad's face at that instant, his face on the tennis court, slack and dull, all the expression socked out of him.

Frannie shivered watching Sukie as that wretched memory surfaced. It took Frannie back to when her father had died. Back to that moment last spring when she'd come to her dad's from school, opened the bathroom door, and found him crumpled on the floor.

Could Sukie have been traumatized? Could Frannie and the goddess, straight-A Sukie Jamieson, who lived with her golden hair and perfect parents in a Barbie dream house, be sisters under the skin? They had nothing in common. Frannie was an artist to the marrow of her bones. She could be fascinated with the interplay of light and shadow on something as ordinary as toast. Frannie was sure that Sukie would watch the light and shadow only under one condition: if she got class credit for doing it.

Frannie had read somewhere that newborn babies don't smile. People call it smiling but it's either a baby's muscles getting used to working or a reaction to something physical like a tummy ache. What she'd seen in Sukie's face, Frannie concluded, was a gas pain that she'd mistaken for emotion.

Sukie, meanwhile, stood silent. Would that vision forever sideswipe her? Was she lashed to the sight of her dad on the court and the grim man's confiding evil words? *Your dad's slime. Never forget it.* Frannie walked away, but everyone else remained rapt, awaiting more details of her mother's fate. "You won't believe what my mom looks like," Sukie babbled. "Like someone punched her."

She would remember and regret her choice of words.

A Funeral Procession

SUKIE spent forty-five minutes doing the mermaid float, a fleet of vanilla-scented candles sweetening the air, her bathwater oiled with a concoction of eau de kelp and coconut. She emerged liquid-calm. But shortly afterward, she felt the jumps return. By the time her hair was dry, they'd spread from her solar plexus down her arms and legs. That's how much she feared showing up at the meeting tonight with her mom and having to take her nose to meet Bobo on Saturday.

Preoccupied with these worries, she'd barely thought about the strange incidents in the mirror, even when she was looking into it. Her imagination had run amok, turned happy fantasies to nightmares, that's all. The night before, in between answering the Final Jeopardy question and finding out she got it right—"Who is Chaucer?"—she'd even had a fit of giggles thinking about her mom, Señor, and herself all screaming at the same time. As for the crack, while it was possible that Señor's piercing scream had caused it, more likely it was the result of age—the mirror was over sixty. Considering that, it was in remarkable shape. The tiny crack was hardly visible. When she stood in front of the mirror, it bisected her ankle, not a high-priority body part.

Now that her cell was back in her possession (and her racket too—delivered by the club's lost and found), she summoned Bobo's texts to enjoy them again and again. MEET ME AFTER THE GAME. DANGER CATION. She'd texted back, SEE YOU THEN. The brevity evoked mystery—or so she believed until she hit send, when the truth clubbed her: It was bland. Her golden hair and even her creamy complexion were a front. Underneath she was one hundred percent beige. She wished this truth were deep underground, but she suspected the opposite. It was right out there, and only Sukie had been too blind to see it. "Beige Girl. You are Beige Girl," she tortured herself in the mirror.

"Why does Mikey have to come tonight? He's not going to college," she said, although she didn't really care.

"Because I forgot to get a sitter."

Her mom lay on her back in her underwear as she pulled on tight pants that showed every curve of her shapely legs. On her bed on her back was the only way she could put on pants without bending over, an act that was positively forbidden. As Sukie watched, standing in the doorway of her parents' bedroom, she squeezed the flesh on her arms, working her way from her wrists to her biceps. Again and again she squeezed, trying to quiet the jumps.

"What are you doing?" asked her mom, sitting up carefully.

"Nothing." Sukie stopped, but she started squeezing again a minute later.

"As soon as I get all my expressions back, I'll teach you how to cry on command. It can be useful. Put that on me, would you?" She nodded toward a silk top draped on the chair and raised her arms like a little kid. Sukie dropped the blouse over her mom's head. Her mom adjusted the shoulders and slid her feet into flats. "Now pull me up slowly." She extended a hand.

Ever since she'd come home, Sukie's mom had moved in slow motion. She never turned her head without at the same time turning her shoulders and chest. "Mom's a robot," said Mikey. Now she squatted slightly to pinch her scarf off the ottoman. Mikey pointed the cable remote at her and emitted simulated sound waves—"eh-eh-eh-eh-eh"—as if he were controlling her movements.

Her mom swirled the scarf around and around, up her neck, over her chin, to just under her bottom lip.

Sukie handed her a black felt hat. Studying herself in the mirror, her mom adjusted the brim low and slipped on her enormous dark glasses. "Ta-da," she said.

"In case anyone asks, I think we should all say I had a bumper stumper," her mom announced as they drove to the school.

"What's that?" asked Sukie.

"Oh, you know, a mini-accident. I rear-ended someone and banged my nose on the steering wheel."

"I already told them something," said Sukie. "I meant to mention."

"You did?"

"Yes."

"What did you say?"

"I said you had a spa accident."

Her dad burst out laughing.

From the back, Sukie saw her mom turn her head and shoulders stiffly toward him. "What's funny about that?"

Her father shrugged.

"I said you dove into the shallow end so, I mean, if anyone says they're sorry about the accident, you'll know."

"For sure," said her dad.

"What's that supposed to mean?" said her mom.

"Don't," Sukie blurted.

"Don't what?" asked her mom.

Have a fight, Sukie was thinking, but she knew to shut up.

"Darling, is something on your mind?" Darling was not darling. Darling was the opposite of darling. Darling was a dagger thrust between the ribs.

"Lay off her," Sukie's dad said mildly.

"You two are in it together," said Sukie's mom. "Am I right?"

No one bit on that.

Her dad pulled into the right lane to join the slow-moving line of cars entering the school lot. A funeral procession, thought Sukie. I'm on a trip to my own grave.

Cobweb

THE funeral idea took root. By the time they'd parked and her mother had fluttered waves to several other parents, Sukie had decided to play corpse for the evening. I possess no feelings, she told herself. Pain nor pleasure, hurt nor joy. I am beyond all mundane earthly emotions, and while present am absent.

She had dawdled, letting her parents and Mikey go ahead. Her mother had fussed about not having a pad and pen, fumbling through the messy glove compartment. "What's this?" she'd said, holding up a DVD receipt. "*The Other Boleyn Girl*? Who watched that?"

Her dad, who would normally be striding about

glad-handing, waited by the open car door, pointed to the brightly lit cafeteria, and said only, "I guess that's where we go." They set off on their mission to get their daughter into the best possible college, strung so tight that they didn't notice that the object of their concern, Sukie, wasn't with them.

Face dulling was called for. A slack jaw, limp cheeks, loose lips, shallow breathing. Only enough air to sustain motion must enter system. She felt like Mikey, making up robot rules, only hers were for the walking dead. Alone in the backseat she experimented on the front-seat headrest. "Orbs aslumber," she intoned. Soon, without being closed, her eyes lost focus. The headrest was no longer a headrest but an identity-less padded object.

She took a selfie and studied it. Did she look dead or merely stunned (as if someone had tapped her lightly with a mallet)? She couldn't tell, because the photo was too dark. She was cloaked in shadow. There is a zombie truth, she thought, and I am it.

She stepped out of the car.

A sparring wind slapped her pants and blew open her pea coat. She struggled to button it and keep the collar turned up chicly. "Wind, you can't defeat me," she whispered. "Cold, you fool, I am beyond shivering." She might be channeling Ophelia and Shakespeare's way with words. Maybe. For sure. For sure maybe. She aimed for grace. She would be a beautiful and arresting corpse. No. She would be a nomadic angel—that had more allure. In the midst of classmates and their parents, she observed without connecting. The role suited her because Sukie often had to pretend that she was actually a part of things. Attaching herself to existing groups, she commented, laughed along with everyone else. *If I leave, no one notices or cares,* she had noted in her journal. *No one goes "Oh, God, no, where's Sukie?"* Tonight she would enjoy her invisibility. Choose it rather than have it be her fate.

The parents conversed in hushed tones, and she could hear Mr. Vickers's hearty greetings. "Come on, don't be shy, it's no big deal, your child's future is at stake, that's all.

"What are you going to do with this bag of bones, haw, haw, haw," he said, referring to lanky Troy Bascomb, who was duking it out with Sukie for the most A's and was such an extraordinary fencer he was trying out for the Olympics. "Your very existence is an embarrassment," he assured Jenna's parents. He even elbowed Dr. Fusco, Autumn's dad, a man everyone was terrified of. Dr. Fusco did brain surgery. "Where's your kid?" Mr. Vickers asked him. "Hiding in plain sight like all the rest of them?"

Trying not to see, Sukie actually perceived more keenly. She knew what Vickers meant. Kids lagged behind parents and, as quickly as possible, migrated to friends. Denicia bolted from her mother's car as if she were escaping kidnappers.

Sukie, at the back of the crowd, spied her tall dad at the front. If she'd craned, she could have seen her mom, too, but the dead don't crane. At most they mill about. "Well, if it isn't the parents of the driven and studious—" Vickers abruptly shut up.

Had he forgotten her name?

"—Susannah Jamieson." There. He supplied it.

She knew what had happened. Her mother's face. Vickers had been temporarily silenced by the close-up truth.

Did the dead have parents? She made up another rule: No parents for dead people. Tonight she was an orphan.

There was no escaping Vickers, however, because she had to pass him to get in. "How are you?" He dropped his goofy cheer and peered down through rimless glasses. She responded with a bland vague affect. He pressed her arm. "Are you all right, Sukie?" She shrugged and floated by. "How's Emma?" he barked.

Emma? Who was Emma? Even if she'd cared, she couldn't ask. Speaking broke the rules, as did caring. In fact, it occurred to her, the dead didn't have teachers either.

"I'm referring to Madame Bovary." He cupped his mouth and blared into the cafeteria. "All you kids in AP English, don't forget. Settle on your topics. Essay presentations begin a week from Monday."

Sukie's mom had staked out a front-row table, laying her coat across the bench on one side and propping her purse prominently on the other. Sukie drifted as fast as zombie legs could drift in the other direction, past Mikey with a fistful of cookies, over to the refreshment table, where Jenna's boyfriend, James, was peeling oranges.

"You will not believe this orange James discovered," said Jenna. She offered samples, passing slices on a paper plate soggy with juice, standing on one leg while she did it. Jenna was, Sukie observed, excruciatingly graceful. Sukie sometimes thought there was nothing she couldn't be jealous of, even an ability to raise your leg and point your toe while serving orange slices. Jenna was studying ballet and Sukie wasn't, but still. James, meanwhile, a serious foodie, spun an orange in one hand and wielded a small paring knife with the other. The peel fell off in a perfect spiral.

"A surprisingly huge variety of oranges are grown in Sicily," said James.

"You're the professor of fresh fruit," said Frannie.

"You are." Jenna giggled. She popped a slice into his mouth and mopped juice off his chin.

He started skinning another. "They're called Moros." He glanced up and flinched.

"What's wrong?" Jenna asked. "Are you all right?"

He sucked his knuckle while he stared at Sukie.

Did I make him nick himself? wondered Sukie. Is that a compliment?

"Given what we pay in tuition, you'd think the refreshments would be better."

Sukie realized her dad was standing next to her, his bad side showing. As he popped a cheese cube into his mouth and chewed, the lumpy purple bruise on his cheek pulsed.

Autumn's mother, pouring juice, nudged Ethan's mother, who was upending a plastic bag of prepeeled baby carrots, the kind Sukie's mother refused to serve because they looked like stumps. In an obvious way that was supposed to be subtle (Ethan's mom scratched her head and Autumn's feigned a yawn), they both considered him and then pivoted to view Sukie's mom, now sitting quietly with one arm bent so her hand happened to block her face. But it didn't. Anyone could see the hideous swelling, the bruising at its ugliest (involving yellow), and bits of the nose bandage. Sukie struggled to keep all expression washed from her face. Her parents matched. They went together in the worst possible way.

She looked around. Nearly every person at the college prep meeting in the Cobweb cafeteria was finding an unobtrusive way to check out her parents. Ethan interlaced his fingers and stretched, peeking between his arms.

She looks like someone punched her.

Sukie's own words came back to her.

Like someone punched her.

Sukie had been so focused on her mom, she'd forgotten her dad.

She looks like someone punched her.

Yes, she did. Like Sukie's dad had punched her and she'd punched him back.

The bars of lights striping the ceiling, lights that exposed every one of the seven grains in the bread that health-conscious Cobweb insisted on using for students' sandwiches, also exposed Sukie's mom as a battered wife.

No wonder Vickers had detoured into sincerity at the sight of Sukie. The knuckle-sucking incident made sense now too. James had cut himself when he'd caught sight, not of Sukie, but of her dad standing behind her. Everyone saw the spa accident for the lie it was, and everyone knew about it because it was such a terrific lie, so juicy that it had spread through Cobweb like wildfire.

Now the entire class thought they had discovered a hidden truth, only that truth was a lie too.

Curiously and confusingly, in this lie that everyone believed—that her mom was battered and her dad the batterer—her dad came up slime. Slime again. How ironic, how spooky, how strange.

Sukie's arms popped with electricity as the jumps shot through her. She forgot her zombie disguise, sidled along the wall to the back of the cafeteria, and huddled at a table alone. Fortunately Mrs. Dintenfass, the guidance counselor, waved her arms, tapped the microphone, and announced it was time to begin. Parents quieted instantly, found seats, and started shushing kids who didn't get how unbelievably important this meeting was.

"It's vital that your children distinguish themselves not only academically but in their extracurricular activities," said Mrs. D.

"Basically, colleges are looking for well-rounded students who are quirky and offbeat," said Mr. Vickers. "In other words, it's impossible to please them, so why try?"

Parents laughed loudly, although the remark was barely worth a chuckle. They needed to laugh because they were wrecked with worry. Sukie laid her head down on her arms.

Someone poked her.

She turned her head and opened an eye. It was Mikey.

"Did Dad hit Mom?" he asked.

"No," said Sukie.

He nodded.

"But some people think so." She flopped up and slid over so he could sit.

The questions at the meeting were endless. How many AP classes did Andrew need? How many times should Moira take her boards? Is it a good idea to have SAT tutoring? Safety schools? Soccer scholarships? "Keep your chins up and your Facebook pages clean," Vickers said at one point. "Merely a life tip, nothing to do with college." Kids and parents were fighting too. Frannie's mom asked, "To maintain your career options, do you think it's better to go to a liberal arts college?" and Frannie shouted from across the room, "I told you I'm going to art school," and her mom called back, "I was just asking a question," and Frannie shouted, "Don't."

"I'm not going to college," said Autumn. Her father stood up and said, "Excuse us," and they left.

Sukie's parents hunted her down the minute the meeting was over. "Tell me again what you're doing," said her mom. "Besides school."

"Tennis, flute, EGG."

"What's EGG?"

"Educating Girls Globally. We're having a festival to raise money for girls in India."

"India?" her mother considered. "Africa would be better."

"India's fine," said her dad.

"You don't want to come up short. It would be awful if you came up short."

"I'm on the debate team."

"That's a good one," said her dad, while her mom beckoned, wiggling her finger. When Sukie leaned in close, she murmured, "You are the most amazing person here. You are better than everyone. Isn't she better than everyone?"

"Better than everyone," her dad agreed.

Was she better than everyone or doomed to come up short? Or both?

"Sukie, wait." Mrs. Dintenfass waved. She was surrounded by parents, and after several comforting pats and verbal assurances that they could call her office at whim, she finally was able to tell Sukie, "Your tutoring starts next week."

"I'm being tutored?"

She laughed gaily. "As if you needed it. No, you're tutoring. An eight-year-old boy. Don't you remember? We talked about it in the library."

So that's what she'd agreed to.

"Tutoring. Wonderful," said her mom. "Is he underprivileged?"

"No."

"Does he speak English?"

"Yes."

"That's too bad. I think it would be better if it were bilingual tutoring, because any way that you can distinguish yourself, that's clearly the point."

"He needs tutoring because he has a learning disability," said Mrs. Dintenfass. "And he's ADD."

"Oh, good."

"The important thing, Sukie," said Mrs. Dintenfass, "is what do you like?"

Like? It had never crossed Sukie's mind that she was supposed to like something. She was supposed to do well in everything, but like . . . ?

"Like is for later," said her dad. "Trust me on that."

"Well, it would be nice if she liked the things that she does," Mrs. Dintenfass said diplomatically. Because she handled the college application process, she had a poor opinion of Cobweb parents. She saw them at their most desperate and calculating. "So, Sukie, what do you like?"

"Um . . ."

"Darling, think," said her mom. "How hard is that?"

"Tennis. I love to play tennis."

Her mom sighed loudly. "It's all your fault that she loves tennis," her mom told her dad. "She just likes it because you like it."

"No, I really like it."

"What are your friends' hobbies?" asked her mom.

"She doesn't have any friends," said Mikey.

"Shut up," said Sukie.

"Of course she does. Would you like to work in Appalachia this summer? Or Peru?" said her mom.

"Peru or Appalachia?" Sukie was feeling faint.

"She doesn't have to decide now," said her dad.

"Would I have to sweep?"

"Sweep what?" asked her dad.

"Floors."

"I don't know," said her mom.

"I don't want to sweep."

Mrs. D.

THE next morning in the middle of first period, Sukie was called to Mrs. Dintenfass's office. "Oh, Sukie," she said, as if she were surprised to see her even though she'd sent for her. Mrs. D. indicated that Sukie should sit in the chair in front of her desk and smiled at her for what seemed like an eternity while she dunked her tea bag up and down in a mug. The mug featured a drawing of a cat balancing a book on its head. "Would you like some tea?" asked Mrs. D.

"No, thanks." Sukie's leg started to jiggle nervously. She'd visited Mrs. Dintenfass's office several times and had never been offered tea before.

Mrs. D., a thin, awkward person with a narrow face and wispy hair, had, Sukie noted, a sparrow nose.

"Sparrow" was bony, slender, with a slight upturn and a tiny point at the end. Sukie's world was rapidly becoming no more than a collection of noses. On the way to the guidance office she'd passed "bulb," two "Greeks," and "fried egg." The office secretary had "beak."

"Cobweb is family," said Mrs. D.

Sukie nodded.

"Families care about one another, and you are an important member of the Cobweb family."

This is going to be bad, thought Sukie.

"What's going on at your house?"

"What do you mean?"

Mrs. D. opened her hands as if it were self-evident.

"My mom had a spa accident."

"I heard that. What is really going on?"

Sukie studied the small daisy plant on the desk, realizing for the first time that it was fake.

"Susannah, I have known you since kindergarten. You're a wonderful person and a good student, and I'm very concerned. You can trust me. Nothing leaves this room. And neither do you until I hear the truth."

“My mom had a facelift,” said Sukie.

“And your father? What about your father? What happened to him?”

“A man beat him up.” Sukie burst into tears.

Mrs. D. opened a desk drawer, removed a small box of tissues, and held it out. Sukie took a tissue and pressed it against her face.

“Take two.”

Sukie took another.

“Do you know why?”

Sukie honked her nose, wiped her eyes, and wadded the tissues into a ball. Mrs. D. nudged the wastebasket over with her foot, and Sukie, after another loud blow, dropped in the used tissues.

“Do you know what happened exactly?” Mrs. D. prodded gently.

Sukie pulled some strands of hair in front of her eyes and examined them.

“It must have been scary.”

With the light behind them these hairs look white, thought Sukie. Could I be going white?

“So you have no idea why this happened?”

“No.”

“But you saw it?”

"Sort of. Yes."

"Did you ask?"

"No."

She would never tell what the grim man had said. She would take that to her grave. She wouldn't tell even if they strung her up by the thumbs, a torture that Sukie had heard about, but she wasn't sure how it worked.

"Please don't tell anyone about my dad. I promised him." Remembering that promise and that she'd violated it produced another flood of tears.

"Your secrets are safe with me. Don't worry." Mrs. D. pulled six tissues and held them out. "Here, sweetie, take these in case you need them. You can go back to class."

That day Sukie noticed that most kids ignored her more than ever. I don't care, she told herself. I don't need friends. Friends are peasants, a Madame Bovary-ish notion that amused her. During lunch period, while she was eating her tuna-fish sandwich, standing by her locker, she saw Frannie watching from down the hall. Sukie smiled a crocodile smile, gay and full of joie de vivre, she imagined. The football game was only three days away, two if you didn't count today. She didn't see Frannie raise her hand in a tentative wave, because Sukie took out her phone and snapped a selfie while chewing. Eating might be involved. She'd better know what she looked like eating.

The Friday Night Before the Saturday

TO give "Meet me after the game" a romantic aura, Sukie called it a rendezvous.

"My rendezvous tomorrow with Bobo," she said to the mirror. She placed her palm on her heart and filled her face with sincerity, an activity that required pushing her breath into her cheeks until saliva bubbled up behind her lips.

When a bit of drool broke the mood, she gave herself a strict talking-to. "No expectations."

She decided to make a "flatman." Sukie's mom had taught her this: to select the clothes she planned to wear the following day and lay them on the carpet the night before in the shape of a flatman.

She tried on dozens of things, and, to avoid bad

luck, rehung them all precisely—the collars on blouses and jackets turned down and matching, all shoulders even, jeans clipped so the legs fell to the exact same length. She retied the bow on her scooped-neck blouse six times until it was a vision in symmetry, and reset her shoes side by side neat as bottom teeth.

Everything even, even, even.

Once she'd arranged her selections on the floor and admired the look, she stripped to her bikini underpants, pulled on an oversized T-shirt, and crawled into bed.

Her final task, her karmic task, was to get into the least expecting frame of mind when every cell in her body throbbed with excitement, desire, and hope.

With the whir of the overhead fan providing an accompanying rhythm, Sukie lay on her back repeating over and over, "Expect nothing, expect nothing, expect nothing." Eventually the recitation of the impossible-to-achieve mantra put her to sleep.

Señor

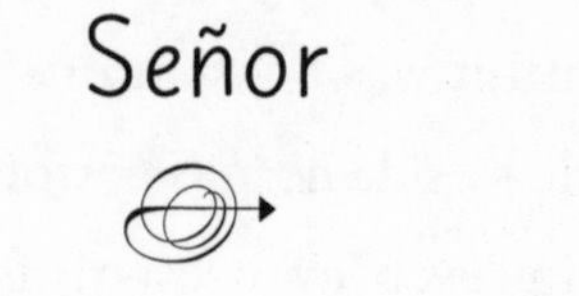

SUKIE had a clock inside her. When she set her alarm for seven, she knew she would wake up just before it went off, and on Saturday morning she did. At six fifty-eight. Sheets of rain slammed the window, a madman trying to break in. Rain. She shot up in bed, swung her legs over the side, hopped down, and saw Señor lying on her flatman.

Señor had never lain on her flatman before.

She rubbed her hands over her face. "Señor," she moaned.

He rolled over.

That turned her bug-eyed. Señor never rolled over. It was a complete 360-degree roll. And furthermore, while on his back, he undulated, a horizontal hula move both sensual and exhibitionistic. When he stood up, he'd left her entire flatman creased, flecked with white hair, and smudged with dirt. Señor might have spent half his life self-grooming, but he was still a dog.

He'd rolled over.

"Roll me over" was Bobo's first message. Did Señor know that? How? Was this a joke? Was he teasing her? He'd teased her mom by nudging his red ball off the second-floor landing. And what about the mirror? There were several more fissures now, long spidery cracks that had splintered off the first. Was the weakened mirror slowly cracking up? Or had Señor been screaming when no one was home?

"Sound waves vibrate at a lower frequency inside a glass than outside, and when a person hits a high note, that tension causes a glass to shatter," Sukie told Señor. "But a mirror isn't a vessel, so how are you pulling this off?"

The mirror rattled, reminding her—rain, Bobo, late. She leaped over Señor and jabbed the start button on her computer.

Hurry up, she begged it. She was ten minutes behind schedule. Eleven. Really an hour, maybe three if she included having to decide what to wear all over again (and having to rehang the rejects in a good-luck way). She clicked on Safari. Why was this taking so long? Finally she was able to Google the Weather Channel website and the information she craved: Rain will stop midmorning. Thank God. She bolted to the bathroom.

In the shower she clocked her conditioner at five minutes (using a kitchen timer), the exact recommended time for fortifying and softening, and after rinsing, she toweled herself with her fluffiest bath sheet, which she then wrapped and tucked above her breasts, and began the arduous task of preparing head and hair for Bobo.

She felt damp under her arms and sniffed. She'd left the shower not two minutes ago and was already sweating. Using a washcloth, she sponged her armpits and applied enough deodorant to wax a floor.

BEDHEAD MERMAID. Last night she'd taped those words next to the mirror below the near-poem.

She bent over, let her wet hair hang like a mop, and began blow-drying.

This was grueling work. Patience was crucial because Bedhead Mermaid could be achieved only by drying on the gentlest setting. Her head throbbed as the blood rushed in. Her wrist ached from holding the salon-quality dryer upside down. Gladly she sacrificed. To keep her spirits up, from time to time she whispered, "I am chill." Her head began to feel as heavy as cement.

Whap. Señor tapped his paw into the back of her knee. Sukie's leg buckled. She crashed onto the bathmat, the front of the dryer smacked her forehead. She sat upright and thrust her face at the mirror. She had a semicircular dent, a C curving from her left eyebrow up to her hairline.

Quickly, she squirted ultralite moisturizer into her hand and massaged the dent. "Señor." She couldn't keep the reproach out of her voice. "Señor," she sniffed in despair. But wait. She whirled back to the mirror. Yes, her forehead was creased, it did seem as if someone might have used it for a sofa but . . . but . . . she couldn't help noticing her hair.

It was magnificently messed. That shove of Señor's had been helpful. A smile stole across her face. "My hair is a thicket, wild and thorny." She fixed the mirror with a bold stare. "Toss me that." She threw out her arm and caught a sword somersaulting through the glass into her grip. Was it real? At that moment, her reflection was her creation. "Hold it." With her unoccupied hand she signaled time out and took a second to retuck her towel more securely and wedge her feet into four-inch high heels. These were her favorite shoes. The leather, the color of pink grapefruit, was perforated all over like a doily. She'd always known she would wear these shoes today. No others had been in the running.

She raised her sword. *"En garde."*

Sukie's entire knowledge of fencing came from watching *Pirates of the Caribbean 1, 2,* and *3*. *"En garde,"* "thrust," and "parry" were her entire fencing vocabulary. But when she lunged, her form stunned. She could feel the tension in her spine, her free arm arced elegantly. Faint shadowy reflections in the tile walls morphed into a dense woods. There were thick trees, ancient and gnarled, branches with fat tufts of green hanging as thick as curtains, which Bobo parted, bursting forth to fight the duel. He spun, he leaped, he struck wildly, all in his football gear, which evened the match: him fencing in the bulk and weight of padding, she advancing and retreating in heels and a towel. She nicked him. He froze. He lifted his injured wrist to his mouth, all the while his flashing black eyes pinned her as helpless as a full-frontal tackle. Then with a kick he sprang forward and Sukie, jumping back, rammed into a tree. She raised a high-heeled shoe, stuck it in Bobo's ribs, and pushed. Sliding around the trunk, she escaped to the other side.

"En garde!" she shouted.

Their blades clashed, sending sparks of light floating up and into the night like lost stars. Sukie halted, struck by their magic, and Bobo, with an upward thrust, knocked the rapier from her hand. With the point of his sword at her heart, she sank to her knees.

Still she felt the prick of his blade. "More surrender," he demanded. He flicked his sword at the tuck in her towel, loosening it.

"Are you in there, Sukie?" Her mom rapped at the door.

Sukie, wedged into a corner of the shower, deep in a place ever so much more entrancing and erotic than her own life, scrambled up. "Just a second, Mom." She kicked off her shoes, scooped them up, and stepped out of the dry shower. "I'm coming." She peeked out the door.

She'd forgotten her mother's face.

Since her mom's return, Sukie had aimed her eyes above her mother's shoulder, or into her bangs, or below her neck, or at her ear to avoid the creepy feeling, This is not my mother. The gauzy nose bandage was now replaced by two strips of tape, but her mom's face was still engorged as if several creatures small and swampy had taken up residence under her skin.

"Where are you going?" her mom asked, immediately understanding that Sukie was preparing for something.

"Oh, I have a . . . a bunch of us are meeting at the Hudson Glen football game."

"Who?"

"Oh, you know. . . ." Sukie couldn't think of anyone to suggest. Whom did she ever hang out with? "Bobo Deeb, the quarterback. We're . . . we're friends. I'm meeting him after."

"That's nice."

"I'm hoping Dad can drop me."

"I'm sure he can. I can't. I'm not allowed to drive."

Sukie knew that. Her mom had already mentioned several times that she wasn't allowed to drive for three weeks. Sukie had no idea why her mother couldn't drive. What did steering and pressing the gas pedal and brake have to do with her face? Perhaps simply the sight of her mother behind the wheel might cause an accident.

"He's the quarterback?"

"Yes," said Sukie, pride sneaking in. She shifted her glance to the mirror and noticed a puncture. The mirror had a hole in it. She pivoted, blocking the mirror with her back.

"Don't make that face," said her mom.

"What face?" said Sukie.

"Where your lips go down. If you do that, you'll get deep grooves from here to here." With the edge of her thumbnail she traced a line from one end of Sukie's lips down to her chin, and then did the same on the other side.

Sukie forced her lips slightly upward.

"I regret every frown," said her mom. "You can't cut out smiles, that's not practical, but it's better to smile only when you mean it. I regret how polite I am, really I do."

"Mom, I have to get ready. I have to do myself up."

"Of course," said her mom, and mercifully left.

Ramp

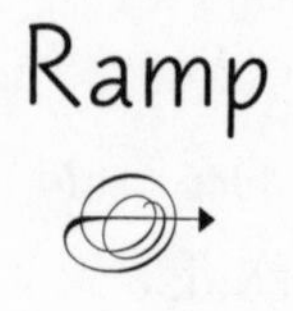

SUKIE examined the hole in the mirror. Had it been there yesterday? This morning? How could she not have noticed it? Had she poked the mirror? With what?

"My beautiful mirror." Sukie, distressed, saw her reflected face full of awful creases her mother had warned against. She tried not to show her upset, to will her features into indifference, but expression (and creases) kept creeping in. "Did you do this, Señor? Somehow, did you?"

Señor rolled on his side and closed his eyes. Conversation was useless. Besides, she was late.

She assembled various liquid bases and experimented. On the first try, she glopped it on her nose as thick as peanut butter. She scraped it off and began again . . . and again . . . and again—patting it lightly, wiping with minisponges, lighter on the sides, heavier on the ramp, striping not blending, blending not striping. Her eyes strayed to the hole in the mirror.

She pressed her body flat against the glass. Such an odd thing to do, she didn't know why the urge came upon her or why she acted on it. The hole in the mirror was approximately at the location of her heart. She stepped back and touched it lightly with her fingers. It was small and perfectly round. For a second she lost herself in fantasy. This puncture was proof—she'd dueled with Bobo in an enchanted forest. The tip of his sword had pierced her heart. Or perhaps it was an omen—the surrender was yet to come.

Stop, she scolded herself, get real, and she returned to the serious problem, her nose. Remixing the makeup, lightening "sand" with a bit of "bisque," she sponged on a few dabs. After viewing her nose in various lights, natural and artificial, she was finally satisfied. She'd neutralized "ramp." She'd successfully doctored her most exotic feature. It was now innocuous. Bland. Finally she was ready to take her nose to meet Bobo.

As for the rest of her face, she kept it simple: six

coats of mascara (letting each dry before the next), lip pencil brightened with a coral gloss selected from a minicompact of four corals mysteriously named Pink Devil. "The devil is in me," she told the mirror before diving into her closet and the problem of what to wear. She made a radical choice: a short red suede jacket with a fringe, something she'd almost forgotten she owned. "Hello, what is this?" she said upon spying it. Solving her nose made her brave, even jocular, and she completed the rest of her choices quickly—skinny jeans, her pink grapefruit heels of course, and snug-fitting layered T-shirts (tawny over tangerine). She blew kisses to Señor as she left. "I love you, I love you, I love you." She was so grateful to him for wrecking her flatman and knocking her to the floor.

"Come in, darling, let's have a look at you," called her mom.

Her parents were in the living room but not together. In her journal Sukie had noted the difference between being together and being in the same room at the same time. Her parents were often the latter and rarely the former. Even when they strolled side by side, they seemed to be in separate spaces. Sukie could assess her parents' moods. She knew, for instance, when her dad was edgy or her mom was "stalky"—looking for a reason to pounce. Her radar was defensive. They would as easily pick on her as each other. She would go right to her room and do homework. Sometimes she ran a bath and did the mermaid float. Occasionally if her parents argued loudly late at night, Mikey crawled into her bed and they both buried their heads under pillows.

Today there was a détente between her parents, a temporary relaxing of tension between battling nations. Her mom, thumbing through a magazine, was tucked into an armchair, curled up like a cat. Her dad had taken possession of the couch. Seated on the center cushion, he hunched over his work papers strewn across the coffee table. At the same time, he wielded the remote, switching back and forth between football games.

"You look beautiful," said her mom. "Pretty enough to be in this." She held up *Vogue*.

"Thanks, Mom."

Her dad looked over now and whistled.

"Your father is taking up golf. He's going to the driving range today. He's sick of tennis. Don't you think you should eat something?"

"I'm not hungry," said Sukie. So her hunch had been correct. He wasn't going back to the club. "Am I still going to take lessons from Vince?"

"Of course," said her mom. "Unless, little copycat, you're switching to golf, too. But you can't because you're committed to tennis. And you're a terrific player. 'Captain of the tennis team' looks a lot more impressive on a college application than 'I golf for fun.' Did you meet him on Facebook?"

"Meet who?"

"This quarterback?"

"No. Dad, come on."

"Is your Facebook clean?"

"Clean? What does that mean?"

"I have no idea. Mr. Vickers mentioned it. I suppose not dirty. Nothing to be ashamed of. Where did you meet him?"

"At the mall. I know some friends of his." A lie but not a big lie. She did know a few of his friends because he'd introduced them to her. "Dad?"

"Did you see that?" said her dad.

"Holding," said Sukie. "Why didn't the ref call it?"

"Atta girl—you never miss a thing." He clicked off

the game and dropped the remote. "I'll get my jacket and clubs and meet you at the car."

"Can we see your Facebook?" asked her mom.

Sukie hurried away.

"Susannah!"

"I'm not on Facebook."

"What do you mean you're not on Facebook?" Her mother sprang from the chair.

Sukie knew what had happened. The worry of what her daughter might be up to on Facebook had yielded to an even greater anxiety: What's wrong with Sukie that she isn't on Facebook?

Sukie powered on and out the front door. Her mom would never follow. She wasn't allowed to be in the sun for a month, her skin was too tender. Even though the sky today was blanketed with thick dark clouds, Sukie was safe because, as her mom had explained only yesterday, the sun could beam those ultraviolets right through.

From the doorway her mother begged, "Sukie, I'm trying to have a conversation." But Sukie pretended that her mom was speaking to the wind, and the wind would carry her words over the trees and far away.

"Just tell me, sweetie, why aren't you on Facebook?"

Sukie concentrated on managing her spiked heels on the gravel driveway, although for a second she considered turning and screaming, "Because I hate you."

But that wasn't the reason.

She wasn't on Facebook because she couldn't complete the questionnaire. It demanded originality. Even the simplest query. After hours of staring at it empty-headed, she had cruised her classmates. Under religion, Autumn had written, "Found God in prison." How brilliant was that? Frannie's favorite movie was foreign. Really foreign, like Italian. *Il Postino*, it was called. Sukie had heard her talk about it in school, how sad it was, how much her dad had loved it. Sukie had never even seen a film in a foreign language. How could she confess that her favorite movie was *The Princess Diaries*? And that looming blank . . . the one she couldn't fathom answering: Favorite Quotation. Sukie's head had nearly crashed down on the keyboard at the sight of it. She had no idea what to put, but everyone else did. Even Jenna, who didn't seem deep-deep, only average deep, had a great quote. Sukie had copied it down. "We should consider every day lost on which we have not danced at least once." Friedrich Wilhelm

Nietzsche. James had quoted himself. "Broccoli is better overcooked." Was that even true? Sukie had no idea. Plus, who cared about broccoli, but didn't that make his quote even more inspired and unique? Even drippy Ethan had an Ethiopian proverb. Ethiopia was not the coolest place to have a proverb from, but still the quote was interesting and political, just like Ethan. "When spiders unite, they can tie up a lion."

But the worst part of Facebook were the photos. Everyone posted photos of themselves having fun. With friends.

Her dad opened the car door, tossed his clubs over the front seat into the back, and climbed in behind the wheel. "Let's get out of here."

As they backed out, Sukie peered up. Sunlight streamed though a rent in the clouds. "The sun coming out means nothing," she told herself. "Expect. Nothing."

Hawks and Bulls

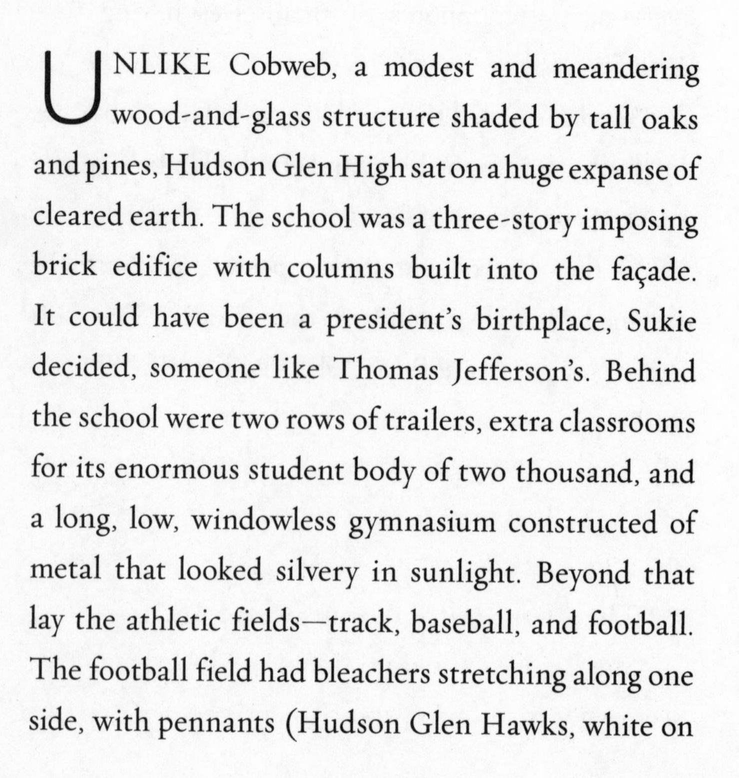

UNLIKE Cobweb, a modest and meandering wood-and-glass structure shaded by tall oaks and pines, Hudson Glen High sat on a huge expanse of cleared earth. The school was a three-story imposing brick edifice with columns built into the façade. It could have been a president's birthplace, Sukie decided, someone like Thomas Jefferson's. Behind the school were two rows of trailers, extra classrooms for its enormous student body of two thousand, and a long, low, windowless gymnasium constructed of metal that looked silvery in sunlight. Beyond that lay the athletic fields—track, baseball, and football. The football field had bleachers stretching along one side, with pennants (Hudson Glen Hawks, white on black, the school colors) rippling across the top.

Swarms of people converged from all directions. Some, like Sukie, had been dropped off in front of the school, others parked in the lot next to the field, and still others arrived from Mason Street, which bordered the opposite side.

Everyone was headed for a good time, and Sukie was one of them.

She didn't mind that she didn't know anyone. It was exciting, like arriving in the city after living one's whole life in a small peasant village. The way Madame Bovary must have felt when she talked her boring husband into moving from Tostes to Yonville, or when she entered the ball at the chateau and the *vicomte* asked her to dance. "I am here to dance with Bobo. Bobo wants me. Hi, I'm here. Hey, well hey. So real. So real life." The conversation she was having with herself was so involving and compelling that she was smiling unself-consciously when, after the long walk, she finally stepped off the asphalt path onto the athletic fields.

The ground felt soft, squishy, spongy.

She hesitated before looking down but then seemingly of its own accord her head fell forward and she saw her shoes. She had stepped onto a patch of grass so soggy from rain that it was nearly liquid, and her shoes were disappearing much the way a car driven into a lake submerges slowly until, with a pop, it's gone.

Faced with this catastrophe and the notion as sudden as a smack on the head that she must solve it immediately or be humiliated for life, her mind froze.

People streaked and streamed about her. She might be no more than a sign on a freeway, one of those innocuous ones like FOOD GAS REST. Girls gossiped in cliques. Friends shared peanuts and popcorn, whapped each other with red licorice vines, shouted orders to pals at the front of concession-stand lines. Some, heads down, worked BlackBerrys. Others nearly knocked Sukie over, so preoccupied were they with their cell conversations. Parents shepherded their children around her. One toddler bounced along, his rain boots making happy smacking sounds on the wet grass. That's when she realized, and how could it have escaped her notice? The foot gear. Every single person wore rain boots or athletic shoes of some sort. They were all prepared for mud.

Only Sukie was in party shoes. Only Sukie.

Was she sinking with no end in sight? Had she located the only square foot of quicksand in the entire United States?

Sukie had been afraid of quicksand ever since, at age five, she'd seen a picture of it in a book, sandy ground and two arms sticking out waving feebly, and no one around to throw a log. Being thrown a log was the only way to get out of quicksand, according to the book. While Sukie rationally knew this wasn't quicksand, she still got blindsided by the fear as if it had been lying in wait for a moment of intense vulnerability to launch an attack.

Wouldn't a friend be helpful right this second? If only she had a friend. A friend would save her. "Hey, Sukie, I'm here, don't worry, I'm throwing a log."

She would hang on to that log for dear life while the friend hauled her and it to solid earth, all the while talking her down. What a comfort it must be to be talked out of panic and to safety by a good friend.

She was deep into the wish for it when she realized with relief that her feet had stabilized, although her heels were so deep in mud that they were nearly as fixed as goal posts. Sukie pulled out her phone and feigned intense interest in nonexistent emails and calls. She pretended for a half hour, until nearly everyone had climbed into the stands and she could see where it was safe to walk. She stepped out of her heels, dislodged her ruined shoes from the mud, and walked lightly on the balls of her bare feet to privacy, the back of the hot-dog stand. Her shoes were dripping and disgusting, all the pretty doily holes clogged. First she wiped them on wet grass, then extracted the little packet of tissues she kept in her purse in a zippered compartment, and used them to smear off the rest of the gunk. When she reached down to clean off her feet, her hair fell into her face. She tried to push it back with her forearm and, when it fell again, used her hand, and soon she had mud and bits of grass on her face. On her carefully sculpted nose.

She slipped her soaked shoes back on, a most unpleasant feeling, and squished along the side of the bleachers. Every time her feet pressed down in her shoes, she produced water. It was as if she were juicing them. They made sounds, too, gurgles, and her feet were numb from cold. She rounded the front of the bleachers. The warmups were over, teams huddled with their coaches for final instructions, some players jumping and twisting, broncos desperate to break out of the pen. She spotted Bobo's number and watched while, for luck, he banged fists with his teammates and trotted back onto the field. "Hey there," she murmured him a hello. "I hope you don't mind my shoes." That amused and perked her up a bit. Cheerleaders and pom-pom girls were performing acrobatically. "Give me an H, give me an A, give me . . ." Sukie yelled enthusiastically, "W-K-S."

Now she scanned to the top of the first set of bleachers. It was overstuffed with fans. Proceeding along, she kept her head down, not wanting to attract attention. People might notice her filthy shoes. At a loud screeching "Woo," she snapped up. Harry the Hawk, all seven feathered feet of him, flapped toward her and with a whoosh enveloped her in his gigantic damp and smelly wings. Terrifying, pitch dark, no air. Just as quickly he released her. The crowd hooted as Harry began reeling drunkenly, kicking up his huge plastic yellow talons and flapping his wings, trying to bat Sukie this way and that. She dodged the bird to great laughter and ran. She didn't stop until, nearly breathless and exhausted, she had climbed high into the second set of bleachers, more sparsely populated.

She edged down a row to an empty spot, realizing when she got there that the seat had a big puddle on it. "Sit your ass down," a man shouted. Sukie twisted around. Right behind her was a beefy guy, naked from the waist up, with six other beefy guys, also naked from the waist up. Weren't they cold? Each had a large capital letter painted on his hairy bare chest. She arched back to read—what possessed her to think she should? For such a good and obedient A-student, any string of letters meant reading was required. "Finster?"

"The quarterback," he said. "Down."

Sukie put her suede purse on the puddle and sat on it. The woman next to her, cradling a plastic container of fried chicken, pinched a leg with a pink paper napkin and offered it.

"No, thanks," said Sukie.

"Let me know if you change your mind. Where's your hat?"

"I don't have a hat."

The woman pulled a green cap from under her arm and put it on.

"Bobo's the quarterback. Bobo Deeb." Sukie turned to enlighten the painted man who leaped up, shrieking with glee. She wheeled back around. The Hawks had kicked off and the Poughkeepsie running back was tacking skillfully through the Hawk defense. Everyone stood and screamed until he was finally tackled after a gain of twenty yards. Sukie, depressed by that, was the only person who sat down immediately. Folks slapped palms over Sukie's head, reaching up, down, and around, before settling on the bench again and launching a chant: "Bulls, Bulls, Bulls."

It was then that she noticed all the green caps. They dotted the rows below. In front of her bleachers, cheerleaders bounced up and down in green skirts and white sweaters. "Bulls, Bulls, Bulls." A baton twirler tossed her green baton into the air. The paint on the half-naked men's chests was green. She was sitting in the wrong stands. She was sitting with the enemy. With the fans of Poughkeepsie High.

Sukie shrank. She simply deflated. It was as if she took up no more space on that bench than a wrinkled balloon. All her positive attitude, although tempered with "expect nothing" but still leaning positive . . . now gone. She couldn't relocate, it was too late, too traumatic—her shoes, the possibility of another encounter with the giant bird. Besides, that first set of bleachers for Hawks fans was packed to capacity.

She watched the entire game in silence, barely moving. Barely, it seemed, breathing. Not once did she get to shout, "Go-Bo, Bobo." It would have been weird, surrounded as she was by Bullmania, maybe even dangerous. The half-naked man behind her might bean her with his Bull-light, flashlights all the Bulls fans carried. They aimed them at the field and one another, even though it was afternoon and the lights didn't project. Were they morons? Idiots? Sukie entertained herself with thoughts of their low IQs. How understandable, even inevitable, that she would blame them for something she felt about herself. She was the truly stupid one, sitting in the wrong stands. Not only couldn't she cheer Bobo, but she had to sit there meekly when the crowd around her heaped insults on him. "Boo-hoo Bobo" and "Bobo Boob-O." She had to swallow a gasp of fear when the entire Bulls front line rushed and crushed him. One by one his tormentors rose, until only he remained facedown in mud. It was a frightening wait for Sukie until Bobo pushed himself to his knees and, shunning assists from his teammates, finally stood . . . frightening not only because he might be hurt but also because, if he was hurt, he wouldn't be able to meet her after. He'd be at the hospital being rolled into a CT scan machine. At one point a man poked her and said, "Hey grass-face, why so sad, we're going to win." And they did. At the very last second, the Hawks blew a field goal and the Bulls beat them, 21–19. She was sad for Bobo and sad for herself. Grass-face? Was there grass on her face? How could she take a selfie to find out? Not in front of these people. Besides, there was no way to get into her purse. She was sitting on it, the metal buckle jamming her butt.

She stayed put until everyone else had left. She thought about going home, about whether to call her dad to pick her up, but Bobo had had such a hard time, losing in a squeaker. If she stood him up, how cruel would that be? She had to show up for their rendezvous. She owed it to him.

In the privacy of the empty bleachers, she took a selfie and discovered grass blades speckling her face, mud on her forehead, and her nose makeup streaked.

Her suede purse was soggy and one side was discolored. Although it was a shoulder bag, she dangled it from her hand, grasped so that the good side faced out, and trekked down out of the stands. Carefully selecting solid earth, she made her way to the gymnasium, stopping first at a place she'd sworn she'd never enter, a Porta-Potty. There she quickly cleaned herself up, smoothed her nose makeup, freshened her lip gloss, and spoke as confidently as she could to her reflection in the small blotchy mirror hanging over the molded rubber sink. "Hi, Bobo, you played a great game. Great. Great." She tried that word several times. It kept sounding fake and forced. "Great!" Finally she managed to infuse it with a lively energy.

Outside the locker-room door, the atmosphere was grim. Parents slumped listlessly on concrete benches. As more showed up, they greeted in ways that acknowledged the grief: faint nods, half smiles, limp waves. Their younger children—siblings of players—quickly tired of the sadness and moved on to chasing, pushing, and complaining. Could they go to McDonald's and how soon? Adults who conversed spoke softly, and Sukie, straining to eavesdrop, discovered that the Hawks had lost three consecutive games and were therefore out of the running. For what, she wasn't sure, she presumed the league championship. The entire pep squad, about twenty girls, comforted one another, hugging, a few wiping tears.

Sukie stationed herself a little apart but in view of the locker-room door. Bobo could easily spot her. She didn't want to tax his brain and make him dig her out of the mob after he'd suffered so. No flirty hide-and-seek game, it wouldn't be appropriate. Close by, four heartbroken cheerleaders discussed Hunters, the kind of rain boots that Sukie owned but unfortunately hadn't worn.

"I think my boots are too big."

"Meg, you have to buy a size smaller."

"No, two sizes smaller," said another. "I bought a six and normally I wear an eight. God, this is tragic." Her eyes fixed on an empty spot in the distance, and darkened as if she were absorbing the horror of the Hawks loss all over again. Her friends gazed with her into the bleak.

"They're sold out at Gilroy's," said Meg after a moment.

"They still have some at coolboots.com," said Sukie.

Meg cruised Sukie from her bedhead down to her grass- and mud-stained heels, then flicked up to Sukie's face again.

Sukie tucked a hand under her hair and flipped the ends up.

Meg slipped off her velvet scrunchee. Her straight chestnut hair dropped to her shoulders. She pulled it up, smoothed the sides, and refastened it.

By way of a reply Sukie threaded her fingers languorously through her waves, lifted them into a curly nest, twisted them together, and then, in a maneuver requiring excellent coordination, simultaneously tossed her head and opened her hands. Her hair tumbled loose and cascaded.

Meg blew upward at her bangs.

Bang blowing, that's what she tries to top me with, Sukie thought with disgust. No one can beat me in a hair-off. She pushed her thick, tangled, golden locks from one side of her head to the other and then, while they all watched gaga (at least that was her impression), she pushed it back. "Is this where the team . . . ?" said Sukie. "I'm meeting Bobo."

A girl stopped picking at her pom-pom to crush a cigarette under her heel and pass the word to other kids who were standing there. "She's meeting Bobo."

"You're in the right place," said one of the cheerleaders. A single sequined heart-shaped earring dangled as low as her chin.

"Thank you," said Sukie.

The girl with the single earring pulled her sweater away from her chest, stretching out the neck, looked in as if to see if her breasts were still there, then patted her sweater down again. "We're all meeting Bobo." She giggled.

Sukie thought this was really competitive of her and couldn't think of a thing to say back, so she simply pushed her hair again. That will shut her up, she thought.

"Hawks," someone shouted.

The gymnasium door had opened and the team poured out in a steady stream while everyone chanted, "Hawks, Hawks, Hawks." Even though they were all saying the same word, it sounded ragged, unsynchronized, and without punch. "Where's Bobo?" she heard Meg ask.

"Blow-drying," a guy answered.

Blow-drying was not how Sukie imagined Bobo.

She might spend an hour upside down, her arm killing her from the weight of the dryer to achieve a look of unkempt nonchalance, but she liked to think that Bobo shook his wet hair and let it be. The way he had in the mirror. He'd strolled out, his hair still wet from the shower, and shaken his head like the cutest dog before he'd spied Sukie backlit by a blazing sunset.

Where was her scorching sky this evening? Where were the flames of crimson, purple, and rose that set her off to perfection? I don't look good in gray, thought Sukie, noting that the rain was threatening to resume and the dull slate clouds above would do little to enhance her complexion.

She had to accept that the sun was shut out of the story. Tonight there would be no sunset. Not even a mysterious compelling twilight. She had to live with the gray, but not with a blow-dried Bobo. She dismissed the notion out of hand. The guy who'd said it must have been joking. Or jealous.

By the time Bobo finally turned up, the chanting had petered out. He hesitated in the doorway, the image of misery framed. His luscious mouth turned down, his eyes barely open, his posture more slump than slouch. Slowly he raised his hand, knotted it into a fist, and thumped his cheek repeatedly.

I barely recognized him, Sukie confessed later in her journal. *Defeat was transforming. Also the hat.*

She'd seen this kind of hat before, in a movie probably, but didn't know what it was called. It was tweed, with a narrow brim and a sharp crease at the top. He wore it tipped back so that his whole face showed and his thick, black, possibly blow-dried hair flowed in a neat wave across his forehead. The sight of him produced a smattering of applause and a few feeble "Go Hawks." The greeting drove Sukie nuts. It reeked of pity. He deserved better than that. She also felt a weakening in the pit of her stomach. Even miserable, he was magnetic.

Robert "Bobo" Deeb thrust his hands into his pockets and shuffled out. Before he had a chance to buzz the fans and pluck her from them, the four cheerleaders she'd talked to swooped in and surrounded him.

"Bobo," Sukie ventured timidly. When she got no answer, she summoned more courage. "Robert," she called. "Bobo?"

Meg said, "Someone wants you," and the group unfolded enough to allow him a glimmer of a view. He wiggled his shoulder and screwed up his face.

"What's wrong?" the girl with the single earring jumped to ask.

"I itch." His face, turned toward Sukie, showed not a spark of recognition. With his lids so low, Sukie guessed that she might appear blurry.

"Sukie," said Sukie, helping him out.

The girl with the single earring scratched his back.

"Down, over," he said.

"You texted me," said Sukie. "We met at the mall."

The cheerleaders reclaimed ownership, reassembling around him, shutting off any possible response, and moved him along like bodyguards. Sukie called, "I'm sorry about the game. It was the ref's fault."

Bobo stopped.

He side-armed Meg and one of the other girls, moving them over so he had a wide, clear view of Sukie. She charged on. "Kigelburg's foot was in bounds when he caught your pass. The linebacker knocked him out after. That ref is blind. I bet someone paid him, because you would have had a first down there and probably a touchdown, and you wouldn't have even needed that stupid field goal at the end."

Bobo nodded and said the following words as if fighting off a great fatigue. "You got that right."

The crowd erupted. The ref. The ref screwed them. Players, fans, the pep squad, parents dumped every insult, every four-letter word they could think of on him.

I did that, she wrote later. *I put it all in perspective, and it was a really scary thing to do. I mean it was that lousy ref's fault, but I don't know how I had the nerve to come out and say it. I guess Bobo had been so emotionally and physically battered that I didn't think of myself. It was one of those moments when a woman goes for it or not. I went for it and I am very proud.*

"Are you coming?" Bobo asked her.

Go home, thought Sukie, and she did the opposite.

"I ignored my gut," she told Señor, pausing from recording events to consider the moment when she could have done one thing and instead did the awful other, and all that it led to. "Oh, Señor." She buried her head in his fur. Normally he didn't allow much contact, a scratch on the back or two, an ear rub. If someone tried anything more intimate, he would get up, move over just far enough to be out of reach, and resettle. But tonight he simply continued to chew his rawhide. Sukie loved Señor's gnawing, the single-mindedness of it, how he didn't stop until the tough hide was a juicy pulp.

She wrapped her arms around him. Except for freeing his head to chew more comfortably, he allowed the hugging too. This was a turning point for him.

They say that dogs know what's coming. All natural disasters, earthquakes, tornadoes, storms—they feel the earth's tremble, sense electricity in the air before tragedy strikes. Señor had those sensors about the Jamieson family. He knew what was coming before anyone, even before those who would cause it.

Bobo

SEÑOR sat up. His nose twitched, not rapid little sniffs to soak up the savories, but more investigative.

There was someone on the stairs.

Her dad. It had to be. Her mom had taken half a Vicodin and gone to bed ages ago. Quickly Sukie reached for her bedside lamp and shut it off.

A sudden rattling shudder. The hall table banged the wall, Sukie guessed. Her dad had stumbled into it, either because he'd had too much to drink or he hadn't bothered to turn on the hall light. *He won't come in, he'd never come in, don't let him come in.* Relieved, she heard her parents' door—the knob turning and then the click as it was pulled shut.

Señor flopped down and resumed gnawing.

Easing open the drawer in her side table, Sukie located one of her favorite objects—a pen with a built-in flashlight. She did the things she needed to combat the jumps—plumped a pillow, sat up straighter, balanced her journal on her knees, and, most important, continued to write, hoping that if she did, the jumble of thoughts and confusion and agitation would leave her head. The obsessive replay of events might stop. If she dumped her pain into her journal, perhaps when she shut the book, she'd find at least a temporary respite, enough calm for sleep.

She returned to the defining moment. *Go home, my gut ordered,* she wrote in her journal. *I knew I should, but I didn't.*

Sukie trailed along behind Bobo and his girl posse to the parking lot and Kiefer's car. Kiefer, who had been with Bobo on the day she'd first met him, nodded at Sukie, but that's all. He drove. Bobo sat in front, and Sukie was crushed in back with Meg, the single-earring girl, whose name was Swan—well, it probably wasn't, but she told Sukie to call her that—and two other cheerleaders, Mandy and Jinx. The whole way to the house of someone named Lionel, Swan reached around the headrest, one hand on each side, and massaged Bobo's shoulders.

The car rolled right over the curb onto Lionel's front lawn.

Sukie, struggling to keep up because her heels kept sinking into wet grass, followed the group past a pretty peach clapboard two-story house where, judging from the drawn shades, no one was home, to the two-car garage in back.

They entered through a side door.

Sukie nearly gagged. The place smelled of car oil and nachos, although there were no cars. The garage had been converted into a place to hang.

"That's so disrespectful." Jinx pointed to a couple making out on the floor, which was covered in dirty industrial carpeting. "It's like God is dead and they don't know it."

Sukie stepped around the writhing couple and into the crush of gloomy brooding kids drinking beer. Although the mood was funereal and no one talked much, losing hadn't affected anyone's appetite. No sooner did one of the pep-squad girls squeeze swirls of cheese onto corn chips and nuke them than kids scooped the sticky mess up with their hands and licked them clean.

Bobo sank onto one of the two lumpy couches, listed sideways, and curled up into a fetal position. He pulled down his hat to cover his face.

A boy breaking up a six-pack offered a can to Sukie. She popped the top, spraying her shirt with beer.

"Aw, you're all wet," he said. She tried to laugh but coughed instead.

"What's your name?"

"Nothing," said Sukie.

Nothing. My name is nothing?

The boy studied her a minute, took a gulp of beer, and said, "Let me know if you get drunk."

She shook her head yes, then no.

He moved on.

She couldn't figure out how to stand. She tried the way her mother had taught her, with one foot in front of the other. She pretended she was at ease, forcing curious looks onto her face as if the room were filled with things she appreciated. How darling are those red lightbulbs stuck in every socket? Don't they impart a lovely radioactive glow to one's complexion? I love it that I'm standing alone, it doesn't bother me, actually I prefer it, actually I don't give a shit. I am a superior being in an alien world. No, in a world of red-faced aliens. That thought tickled her, but only for a minute. Mainly she longed to feel that she wasn't invisible.

She spent some time pulling strands of her hair in front of her face and examining them. Every so often she yanked one out and stuck it in her pocket.

She forced herself to drink the beer too. *Brew, I'm really into brew.*

Brew is a word I have never used in my life, she wrote in her journal, *but throwing it around in my head was a great aid in helping me drink in a natural way something that tastes foul.*

Bobo was still curled up on the couch.

Meg tapped his hat and he batted her hand away.

Swan pressed a cold beer against his arm. He rolled onto his back, his hat slipped off, and he propped himself up enough to take the beer and chug it. He wiped his mouth with the back of his hand, accepted a bag of chips that Swan now offered, and shaking the bag, tossed a bunch into his mouth. He chased them down with more beer. He eats like an animal, thought Sukie with a shiver of thrill. For a second she imagined him crashing through a jungle, twisting off huge tree branches and chomping them. The vision of his mouth full of broken twigs and lush green leaves made her smile, and then unexpectedly her knees weakened. She had to put a hand against the wall to keep from swooning. He's not an animal, he's a wild man. Wild. Wild.

Swan was dusting bits of chips off his shirt when Bobo caught Sukie's eye. He wiggled his finger, beckoning her.

"Me?" Sukie pointed to herself, and Bobo, in that way he had of making his needs known by the slimmest of means, raised an eyebrow in reply.

Sukie approached slowly. He patted the couch, which was covered in a hairy stained fabric of an especially putrid yellow. She sat gingerly on the edge, and he shifted. She felt the curve of his body against her back.

"I'm glad you came," he said.

"Me too." Sukie twisted around to look at him.

His hand lay heavily on his brow as if he were battling a wretched headache.

"Don't you think it smells weird here?" said Sukie.

Bobo took a minute to consider that while Sukie cringed, and berated herself for saying something so lame. He twirled his index finger. She couldn't decipher the meaning.

"Turn back around," he said.

Sukie straightened so that she was no longer looking at him, and while she was wondering why he would ask that, she felt his cool hand snake under her jacket and shirt and press against her bare back.

Her body quivered, and incongruously she found herself faced with a plate of cupcakes offered with a curtsy and a giggle by a member of the pep squad. "No, thank you," said Sukie. His hand snaked higher.

"Your skin. Not too dry, not too oily. Good glands," said Bobo.

"Glands," Sukie repeated weakly, as his hand did what she was wishing it would. It slipped up to her bra and began fiddling with the catch.

Sukie had made out before, at summer camp with a couple of different guys, less because she liked them than because she was curious. Until Bobo she had never been near any guy who made her insides melt.

"Move over." Jinx bounced down next to her and banged her butt against Sukie's, knocking Sukie to the floor. "Oops, sorry," she said.

Stunned by her sudden ejection, Sukie waited for

Bobo to execute one of his minimalist moves, a head tilt or a snap of a thumb, telling Jinx to skedaddle, but instead he rolled over, burying his face in the couch back.

"Hey, Bo," said Jinx. "Aw, Bo." She kneaded his neck.

The rug was wet with beer and littered with chips and cigarette ashes. Sukie looked at her hands. She'd used them to break her fall; now they were covered with disgusting bits of grit. She unfolded her legs, which had somehow gotten twisted under her, wiped her hands on her jeans, and got up. "I need a beer," she said to no one in particular and, spotting a stack, strode over, seized one, popped the top, and took a swig so big she choked.

"Are you okay?" asked Meg.

Sukie nodded.

"Should I pat your back?" Meg smiled. She had a gap between her teeth. Sukie admired it. How daring to have a space between your front teeth and smile widely. Something about the alcohol going to Sukie's head made her realize that, if she were Meg, she would have perfected a toothless smile. She might even have tried to figure out how to talk without having her teeth show. Although that would have been harder.

"There's beer fuzz on your nose," said Swan.

Sukie wiped her hand across her face in that rough way Bobo had. Swan moved her single earring over to poke her tongue through the hole in the center of the heart.

"It was a mass text," said Meg.

"What?" said Sukie.

"The text you got. We all got it."

Sukie played with the beer can, drawing her finger in a circle around the top.

"'Meet me after the game,'" said Meg. "'Danger caution.'"

Feeling that she might throw up, Sukie walked unsteadily to the door and out into the rainy night.

Sukie

IT was a mean rain.

It soaked and stung her all at once.

Sukie plodded slowly, fearful, in a night so dark she couldn't see her own hands.

The garage had no windows to cast a friendly outdoor glow, and in the Hudson Glen residential areas, there were no streetlights. On clear nights skies were spectacular; shooting stars as frequent as Sunday. Her dad even took buyers to view real estate at night. "In this town the moon is a closer," he'd told Sukie. "If I sense hesitation, I let the moon and the stars make my case."

Sukie fished frantically in her purse for her phone. *No moon, Daddy. No stars. Dad, I have to call Dad.*

"'Oh, Mr. Moon, moon, great big silvery moon, won't you please shine down on me,'" Sukie sang in a tiny, tinny voice.

She'd learned the song from her dad. When he sang it, "shine" didn't mean only "shine," it meant, "Make the deal go through." Sometimes he added that in a deep growl, "Make the deal go through," and they all laughed.

"It's bad luck to exploit the moon," her mom had said.

"Phooey," her dad said. "Phooey."

Phooey. Phooey. Phooey. Phooey.

Dad, there's no moon. Dad!

She couldn't find her phone. Her hand slapped about. Nothing crammed into that big wet purse felt remotely like it.

"Oh, Mr. Moon, moon—" She began walking sideways with her arm extended to prevent collisions. "Oh, Mr. Moon—" Suddenly everything lit up bright as day. Sukie had activated motion sensors tucked along the roof of the house.

Feeling as exposed as if she'd been caught naked in the shower, Sukie cowered. The rain pummeled her. On her nose and cheeks, trickles of black mascara mixed with smears of foundation the consistency of wet clay. Her red suede jacket bled onto her pants and flesh. She might have escaped from a horror movie, victim or killer, hard to tell.

Possibly she was crying, but her sense of helplessness was so complete, she couldn't reckon her own misery.

Then, as if someone had energized her with the squeeze of a trigger, she bolted into the street. Abandoning her shoes. Splashing mud. And turned left to the lights and traffic of a main thoroughfare, Hawthorne Avenue. Without waiting for the green, she shot across two lanes of traffic to shelter under a broad gas-station overhang.

At that moment she realized she was still carrying her beer.

She looked around for a trash can.

Even distraught, drenched—her clothes stuck to her skin—cold as a Popsicle, and shoeless, with water pooling around her bare feet, Sukie was incapable of littering. A girl who wanted to mow the ocean couldn't drop something as discordant as an aluminum can onto the landscape, even when that landscape consisted of asphalt and two gas pumps. Her problem wasn't really with littering. While she was all for green and cared almost deeply about global warming—for science class she'd calculated her family's rather large carbon footprint—and while she'd never throw a banana peel out a car window and she'd even occasionally refused plastic bags at the supermarket, nevertheless, speaking strictly with regard to motivation, an obsession with order and a dread of chaos—these were the forces that drove her.

Besides, littering was bad luck. Sukie was convinced of it.

On a night when her luck could not have been worse, and was about to worsen, she still clung to a belief that doing something as simple as being kind to her environment might alter the course of events.

She poured out the beer, figuring the rain would wash it away, and clamped the can under her arm while she yanked her purse wide open, stuck her head nearly inside, and plowed through. Aha, her phone. Thank God, her phone.

She took it out, turned it on, and dropped the beer can into her purse. The phone shivered. A text message. FROM MOM, she read. SOMETHING STRESSFUL.

The text had been left three hours ago.

Sukie debated and then dialed her dad's cell. It

bumped immediately to his voice mail. "Dad." Sukie meant to act collected, but "Dad" came out in a flood of fresh tears.

Dad. How powerful is that word? Love, safety, comfort, succor. Sukie's cry for dad was loaded with every one of those meanings. "I need you to pick me up." She squeezed her eyes to stem the tears. "Please, Dad. I need you." She clicked off and called home, hoping he would be there and that he would answer.

"Hello?"

"Mom?" Sukie's voice quavered but held steady.

"My ear almost fell off."

"What?"

"I was putting on my sunglasses, and you know that part that goes over your ear? Well, it went into a stitch and snagged it. My earlobe was dangling."

"Oh my God, Mom. Are you okay?"

"I practically wasn't. I had to drive, which is against the rules. To the hospital. They sewed it back on, thank God there was a plastic surgeon on duty or I would have ended up looking like a scarecrow. Also my nose is unusually tender for some reason, I must have banged it in my sleep. They rebandaged it, and I have to keep it this way for weeks. Is your father with you?"

"No."

"I can't find him anywhere. He called after golf and said he was going to look at an office building in Croton. Oh."

"What?"

"Nothing. I thought I felt a twinge. Mikey, make this change channels."

"Mom, I'm stuck. I need a ride."

"Oh, for goodness' sakes."

The line seemed to go dead. "Mom?"

"Call a taxi."

Dad

THE rain had lightened to a drizzle and Sukie decided to walk to the mall, a half mile down Hawthorne Avenue. She had twenty-five dollars. Perhaps at the Kmart she could buy a pair of flip-flops and something warm to wear like a sweatshirt before calling a cab.

Fleur's father owned the Hudson Glen Taxi Company, and while he didn't drive one of the six cabs himself, Sukie worried that if she got into a cab in this condition, Fleur might hear of her humiliation. "I picked up a girl who looked like she'd been spit out of a washing machine." "Cliff picked up a girl who looked like she'd been spit out of a washing machine. Lived on Lilac Drive," and eventually somehow or other more details would come out, how exactly was murky, even what exactly was murky, but her fear was profound.

She passed Clementi's. The Christmas lights that twinkled in the window all year round beckoned. Maybe Issy was on duty. "Hey, I got caught in it," Sukie would say laughing, but probably she wouldn't. Probably she'd take one look at Issy's friendly face and cry.

At Kmart she found what she needed, summer flip-flops on sale for $2.99 and a gray hooded sweatshirt, $10.99. After paying, she retired to the restroom and surveyed the damage in the mirror.

With her exhausted, glassy-eyed stare coming back at her, hair soaked and plastered to her head, shoulders so limp she might have been tossed up by a wave and slammed against rocks, Sukie had to admit she looked demented. She peeled off her red suede jacket, determined that it was wrecked beyond salvation, rolled it into a ball, and stuffed it into the trash bin.

The red dye had even stained her neck, an effect so bizarre it could be the mark of an alien. "Are you one of the evil Polyesters?" she asked her reflection, bolstering her spirits with a bit of role-playing and a poke at her mother at the same time. For her mom, polyester was only slightly less agitating than cellulite. She imagined Bobo, bare-chested with the most attractive light sprinkling of body hair. "Prove you're not a Polyester," he commanded. "Show your neck." He ripped off her jacket and top to reveal the truth.

Bobo.

How quickly he'd snuck back into her fantasy life.

She spritzed some sickeningly sweet-smelling liquid soap onto her hands and managed to eradicate the red and restore her normal skin tone.

Two women came in when she was throwing away her layered tops stained beyond redemption. "I'm all wet," she explained needlessly. "What a downpour."

"I like your bra," one said before going into a stall and then calling from inside, "Did you get it here?"

"Does the underwire hurt?" asked the other, sticking her face close to the mirror and picking at a tooth.

"No," said Sukie. "No to both things. I got it at Victoria's Secret."

She felt a tiny bit better getting a bra compliment and having almost a conversation. She bit the price tags off, pulled on the sweatshirt, and slipped her feet into the flip-flops. She walked to the wall and back, five steps, testing them. Flip-flops always hurt for a while from the thong. With an exhale of exasperation, she did what she could with her hair, slicking it back off her forehead and behind her ears, and fastening it with a rubber band she kept in her purse for hair emergencies.

"Cheer up," one of the women said as they left. "You can't fool me."

Sukie hit the air blower, lifted one leg and then the other. Hit it again, turned and poked her butt out under the hot air. After several hits, turns, and butt-and-leg gyrations, she managed to get her jeans dry enough to separate from her skin. While stiff and still damp, at least they were no longer pneumonia inducing.

She put on some lipstick and realized she was starving. She hadn't eaten all day.

Her mom could pay the taxi when she got home. She would spend the rest of her money on a grilled cheese sandwich at Andee's Diner. She'd call the cab while she ate and meet it outside Andee's, which had an exit straight to the parking lot. "That's a plan," she said to herself in the mirror. She clenched her hand in a fist and said it again. "That's a plan."

When Sukie recorded events later, snug in her bed, she stopped here, laid her journal aside, and buried her head in her arms. This was the beginning of the hardest part to tell. She had jumps so severe her legs were bouncing. Señor rested against them, providing warmth, and Sukie lifted her head, heavy with pain and confusion, and began writing again.

Andee's was closed for renovation, and, after calling a cab—twenty-five minutes, they said—I got on the escalator. It seemed as if I were adrift alone on a great ocean liner. I don't know why, but there was something about the way that escalator traveled from one floor to another offering views from one end of the mall to the other that gave me the most unpleasant feeling that by accident I had ended up at sea, the last place I would ever want to be. My mind jumbled with thoughts. How often Mom and I had shopped here from the time I was little. "Try this." She would seize something by the hanger and hold it against me. "Yes, I am brilliant, I am so brilliant," she would exclaim when I tried it on and it was perfect. Mom does have the most amazing taste. She would always quiz the salesladies, "Is this polyester?" And when they'd say no and show her the tag, 100% cotton, Mom would say, "Do you swear? Because if I touch even a fiber of polyester . . ." She never finished the sentence, leaving horrendous near-death possibilities to their imaginations.

Señor's nose twitched, and Sukie stopped writing. Yes, it is ironic that I was thinking of Mom on that escalator, she agreed with him. He continued to hold her gaze. Yes, recalling fun memories, even more ironic—that might even be a foreshadowing, she acknowledged.

MEG. BITCH. SLUT, she printed in large letters and then, after a scolding from Señor—involving baring top and bottom teeth—forced herself to continue on.

Walking toward Joe's Caffeinated, I passed the glasses store where Bobo had picked me up. How rude was he to horn in on my shopping? When she wrote the word *rude*, she found herself grinning. "I wonder if he missed me." Sukie imagined him rolling away from the couch back to discover her MIA, his intense dismay and disappointment expressed by a flick of his tongue or by holding the blink of his eyes an extra nanosecond. *He's one expressive dude,* she wrote, and crossed it out.

"Tell it, tell the rest," she urged herself on. "To face the truth, I have to record what happened in minute detail," she told Señor, and yet no sooner did she begin than she omitted.

She couldn't admit her vanity, how ignorant, perhaps blissfully ignorant she'd still be if it weren't for the fact that after ordering a mochaccino and selecting one of the few remaining bagels strewn about on the shelf, she took a selfie. And it was because of the selfie, because she couldn't see the photo clearly and turned away from the café window to eliminate glare . . . and by the way how surprised she'd been at how nice she looked. I went from "drowned rat" to "fresh from the swimming pool" was exactly what she was thinking when she raised her head and noticed a couple at the back table.

Location. This matters. Sukie had moved from the front of the counter, where she'd placed her order and paid, to the back of the counter near the tables to wait for her coffee. The woman making drinks gyrated to the piped-in music of the Fugees while she worked the espresso maker and poured the foaming milk. Sukie noticed the tip jar. A piece of paper secured with a rubber band said "love"—"love" in thick felt-tip marker script. *I dropped in change,* she wrote, *for good luck.*

She put the bagel down (on a napkin, of course), not important except that's how she ended up leaving it behind.

The tables at Joe's were small and round with Formica tops, stylish in a retro way, with chrome bands around the edges and matching chrome-colored chairs, and at the farthest table, nearly hidden in the corner, a couple had pulled the chairs around so that they were sitting side by side, facing the wall. The man's arm stretched along the back of the woman's chair and then lapped over her shoulder, and the woman had laced her fingers through his. Even with a view solely of their backs, Sukie could see their clasped hands, because every so often they made an appearance, popping up, untangling and tangling again. The woman leaned into the man—there was something about this, the way her body melted into his, that wasn't only sensual but also easy and free. How confident she was that the man was welcoming, and that more than anything else told Sukie that the couple were lovers. The sight filled her with sadness. The disappointment of Bobo, all the unfulfilled yearning, and the loneliness of having not one friend to tell her troubles to finally sank in.

The woman had short wavy black hair, locks were visible as she nestled against his shoulder. Playfully the man mussed her hair, which made Sukie smile even as her loneliness deepened. The man pulled away. "Sure that's all you want, a glass of tap?" he asked, and it was at that moment that Sukie realized she was looking at her dad.

Her phone slipped from her grasp and hit the floor with a clack. She swung back to the counter, yanked her hood up over her head and down over her forehead, then seized the neck strings to jerk the sweatshirt up. It didn't reach as high as she hoped and she ended up with the strings bisecting her mouth, top lip visible, lower lip not. The hood winged out on the sides like the hood of a monk's cloak, shutting off all side vision, mercifully blocking her dad from seeing her and leaving only a swath of face visible head-on—mainly her nose with two panic-stricken eyes above.

"Whipped cream?" asked the counter girl.

Sukie's head bobbled slightly in reply as her dad passed so closely behind her that she felt a stirring of the air. She squatted, felt the floor for her phone, snagged it, and rose up again slowly as she heard his request. "I'd love two glasses of tap."

She assumed her dad was standing not more than two feet to her left, and this was true. She assumed he'd flashed his winning smile, it always produced quick service. She was right about that too. Being so tall, he reached for the water right over the giant jar of chocolate espresso beans. Sukie calculated that as well. A dreadful curiosity, a compulsion to look over and confirm the horror of what she already knew—to torture herself with a second thousand-volt shock—battled with an even greater terror of being seen.

The counter girl capped her drink and set it down.

"Thanks. Thanks a bunch," she heard her dad say.

Sukie made no move for her drink, and the coffee girl, noticing this, stopped dancing and observed. How odd the way Sukie stood there without a twitch, concealed except for her nose poking through the hood like a bird at a feeder and her eyes radiating anxiety. Anxiety can infect an atmosphere so powerfully that it's practically weather. Sukie was producing a storm.

Not certain of her dad's whereabouts, Sukie waited for a sign that he had passed and returned to his table . . . to the woman—that fact she could barely admit. Don't let him notice me, she prayed. God, please, I'm begging you. And he didn't, and later she wondered how he could not have noticed her. How could he not have noticed his own daughter? Soon she discerned his voice, softer now, mingling with the low drone of conversation in the café. "Here you go," he said.

Sukie turned and used every ounce of willpower to stroll out casually when what she wanted to do was run as fast as she could to the other end of the world.

Home

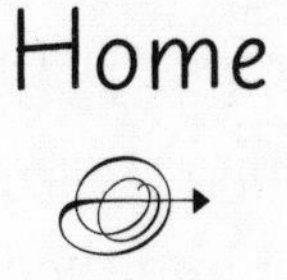

AS soon as I was clear of the café, I ran like hell. It seemed as if I were being chased, that I might be caught, as if I were the one who . . .

Sukie couldn't finish the sentence. The pen flopped from her fingers and rolled off the bed. She was suddenly suffering from an exhaustion so deep, she couldn't write another word.

She shut the journal, toppled sideways, and curled up into a ball. There was nothing more to tell, only tomorrow to dread.

She couldn't recall anything about the cab ride home except hoping that her voice sounded normal when she phoned her mom to tell her she was on her way and didn't have money to pay the driver.

Fortunately her mom seemed preoccupied, like she might have been answering emails at the same time.

Mikey and his friend Tyler, both in yellow slickers, were waiting outside with the money, taking turns walking into trees. Tyler's mom pulled up right behind the cab. While Mikey said good-bye to his friend, Sukie hurried into the house and straight up the stairs.

"Sukie?"

Sukie kept going.

"Sukie!"

"I'm really tired, Mom."

"Stop."

Sukie spun around. From the top of the stairs she looked down at her mom, who had positioned herself in the center of the Jamiesons' grand entryway. Her mother had a heightened sense of space and where she belonged in it. Sometimes, lots of times, she simply hung around like everyone else. At other times, tonight, who knew why, the room was her stage, and while doing something as simple as calling to her daughter, she struck a pose as if she were about to be klieg lit. In her floor-length, ice-pink silk robe (sashed tightly at the waist), holding a glass of white wine, her elbow anchored at her hip, and with the floor, a diamond pattern of shiny black and white marble, radiating out and framing her, she appeared both regal and fragile.

"What is it?" Sukie was surprised to find herself furious.

Her mom waved the wine. It sloshed over. "Oops." She licked the side of the glass. "I just wanted to say hello. Did you have fun?"

"A blast." A blast? Where had that word come from? Sukie had never used it before in her life. "I have to go to the bathroom." She rushed into her room and into the bathroom, and locked the door.

Finally safely home and in a safe and private place, she expected to cry as if her heart were breaking. She even took a hand towel and pressed the soft terry cloth against her face to soak up the tears and muffle her bawls. After a minute of nothing happening, she folded her towel and hung it back up. She peered into the mirror. Perhaps she would find her feelings there, or the sight of her mournful face and sad clothes might trigger them. She felt a pitiful wail rise in her chest, collapse was imminent—but like a sneeze that never quite happens, the moment passed.

The mirror had a new crack, diagonal, higher than the others. It bisected her head from the top center and cut across her left eye at a sharp angle. In the reflection she had three eyes, two on one side of the crack, one on the other. The top of her head had a lump. She moved over slightly. No lump now, but still three eyes.

Her mom rattled the doorknob. "Sukie?"

Sukie flushed the toilet even though she hadn't used it and came out, pushing her mom backward to keep her out of the bathroom. The sight of the cracked mirror would flip her out, provoking expressions and emotions that she was forbidden. She'd blame it on Sukie, and if Sukie had to cope with all that right now, she might beat her mom up. Yes, beat her up. She'd like to punch someone in the face really hard right now. She recognized the feeling only dimly because it was so surprising. She'd shoved Mikey now and then, that's all. Wanting to beat someone to a pulp was not a feeling she was familiar with. But it was there.

"Do you want some dinner?"

"I already ate."

"I made some delicious guacamole."

"No thanks, Mom."

"Do you want to see my earlobe? I have it in a jar."

"What?" squawked Sukie.

"Just kidding. They refastened it." Sukie took note of her mother's newest bandage, a strip of white tape over cotton across the bottom of her left ear. "I was really scared," said her mom in a small voice.

"I'm sorry," said Sukie.

Her mom sucked in her lips.

"Pretty soon I'll be driving," said Sukie.

Her mom nodded. She sat on Sukie's bed. Her silk robe, lightly perfumed with rosewater, clung here but not there in the most flattering manner, and when she crossed her legs, it fell open to reveal her gorgeous calves and most slender ankles. On her bare pedicured feet, the toenails were painted scarlet. "We don't talk anymore," her mom said plaintively.

"Yes, we do."

"No, we don't." She set her wine on the floor, fished a tissue out of her pocket, and dabbed at her eyes. "Tell me something."

"Like what?"

"Something girlfriendy, a secret. You know, confide."

Sukie drummed her fingers against her cheek, then dug her nails in.

Her mom batted her hand away. "What are you doing?"

"Nothing."

Sukie rubbed her neck and snuck her hand up, twisted a few hairs, and yanked them. She curled her fingers around the clump of hair and dropped her hand to her side, all the while feeling trapped by her mother's terrifying request and wistful, watery eyes.

"I don't have any secrets," said Sukie.

Her mom took a sip of wine and studied her. Her eyes sharpened. Sukie began to shudder. She can read my mind, thought Sukie. "Liar. What are you hiding? Come on, out with it, what's that?" She would seize Sukie's fist, pry it open, and recoil from the hairs. "You're a crazy girl," she'd scream. "It's all about your dad, isn't it? Tell me!"

"Is that sweatshirt polyester?" her mom asked.

"I guess so. Part."

"My mother never gave me a compliment. There. I confided in *you*."

"Your mother?" said Sukie.

"That's right. Your grandmother."

"Never?"

"I asked her about it once, just before she died, and she said, 'Well, dear, I tell the truth.'"

"'I tell the truth.' You mean she thought you never deserved a compliment?"

Her mother picked at the duvet, plucking out a tiny feather. "Fly, little bird," she said, and flicked it away.

The sweep of a car's headlights lit the window.

"Is that your dad?" Her mom popped up straighter and slid off the bed onto the floor, knocking her glass over. "Oops," she said. "Double oops." When her mother had had a few drinks, what normally threw her amused her. Instead of a shriek and a dash to the kitchen for some sparkling water to mop up the wine and avoid the catastrophe of a stain, she patted the wet spot affectionately, then planted both her palms on the floor, poked her butt into the air, and pushed herself up with a groan.

"I'm going to bed, Mom. I'm really tired."

"He's on his way. He called from Croton." She padded over to the window and craned over the penguins to look. "Not your dad. Do you want to watch TV with me?"

"I'm tired."

"Come on."

"I got really wet." Sukie hammered each word in frustration and immediately felt guilty.

Her mom lightly tapped the bandage over her ear while her eyes wandered aimlessly around. "Well, this ear kind of hurts. I guess I'll take half a Vicodin and hit the sack. Your dad can cope, can't he? I coped without him. No hugs tonight." Her mom blew a kiss. "Because if even a fiber of that fake fabric touches my skin . . . Look who's here, Señor." She passed the dog as she swayed out.

After shutting her bedroom door, Sukie stripped, pulled on one of her big soft T-shirts, slipped into bed, and wrapped the covers tight.

Her mind was a scramble of things she wished she'd never seen and now she could never forget. Confusions from today mixed with torments from the past. Everything jumbled together randomly, a movie with no clear beginning, middle, and end, no tale unfolding in a sensible comprehensible manner, only an assault of images. That woman's soft swoon into her dad. Her body's comfort with his. The grim man in the red Windbreaker, his grip on her arm, his face shoved forward. The woman's curls of black hair. The way her dad had playfully mussed them. *That's all you want, a glass of tap?* What had the woman worn? Sukie strained but could only recall the chrome spokes of the chairback, although she must have seen a blouse or sweater. Meg's gap-tooth smile. *Your dad's slime. Never forget it.* Was that fearsome man the woman's husband? Or brother? Bobo's cool hand snaking up her bare back. DANGER CAUTION. The mirror cracking—how did it crack, why did it crack? Issy mesmerized by her own twig of a wrist as Sukie's dad held it, his thumb and index finger nearly circling it twice. Did Issy know Sukie's dad was slime? When Issy stabbed her pink hair with a clip, was she considering poking the clip into his eye? Flopman. Did Mrs. Merenda know why Sukie's father got slugged? Did everyone know? Was the charming Warren Jamieson well-known in Hudson Glen for cheating?

Was her dad in love with someone else?

Letting her gaze rest on Señor, curled up by her side, she searched for relief. The jumps were spreading out to the tips of her fingers and toes.

"Maybe the truth can't be buried. Or maybe it can't stay buried. Maybe the very nature of truth is that it will ultimately reveal itself. What do you think, Señor?" And then, in the way that soul mates do, she knew what he was telling her. Until she got it down on paper, she'd never sleep.

She opened her journal, selected black from the packet of various-colored Sharpies, and began to write.

Emma

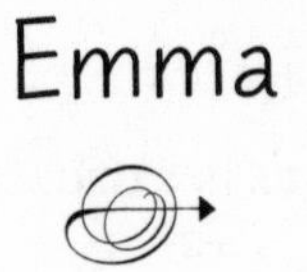

"HEY, kiddo."

Sukie shot up in bed.

Her dad rapped at her bedroom door.

Sukie smacked back down and yanked the covers over her head.

The doorknob clicked. He must have walked in. "Time to get up. It's nine. You have a match today."

Sukie rolled over, squashing her face into the pillow, something she never did.

"Come on, Sukie," her dad said cheerfully.

Slimeball, slimeball, slimeball.

The bed sagged. He must have sat on it. She inched her body away, not wanting him to touch her even through the duvet.

"How was the quarterback?" he asked.

Sukie gave no indication of life.

"Sukie, get up," her mother called, and must have stuck her head in the door because she then asked, "What's going on?"

"I'm clueless," said her dad. "What happened with the quarterback, baby?"

"She was fine when she came home," said her mom.

"Are you sure?" asked her dad.

"Yes, I'm sure. I was here, you weren't."

"Your match is at eleven," said her dad.

"Just Mom." The pillow muffled Sukie's words.

The mattress rose and then sank as her dad got up and her mom sat down. Gently she shook Sukie's shoulder.

"Is he gone?" asked Sukie.

"Yes."

Sukie flipped over and pulled the covers off her head. An assault of light. Morning sun blazed through the window.

"Do you have cramps?" her mom asked.

"No. Yes." She faked an achy voice. "Maybe. My tummy hurts."

"It's the quarterback, isn't it? What did he do? Tell me right now. I won't tell your father."

"It's not—"

"Sukie, you are perfectly wonderful, and if he doesn't like you—"

"You don't even remember his name," snapped Sukie.

Her mom cocked her head as if the name might pop in as a result, and then said, "What does that matter?"

"Bobo," said Sukie.

"Fine. Bobo."

"I'm sick."

"Are you pregnant?"

"Are you crazy?"

Sukie spent the day in bed. She missed her tennis match against Bronxville Prep. It was the first match she'd ever missed.

She began to avoid her dad as much as possible. When he spoke to her, she aimed her eyes over his shoulder or at his knees, or she busied herself with some activity like the computer or her cell. But when he wasn't aware, she found herself sneaking glances. He seemed more changed than her surgically altered mom.

A tweaking of his features, by her own eyes, morphed him from sincere to sinister. Who could trust that smile? It was neither genuine nor ingenuous, but a weapon, a means pure and simple for getting his way. She was suspicious of his sympathy, his ability to engage with and solicit confidences from strangers. Was it an exercise in vanity?

Where she'd seen spontaneity she now saw only performance. "I bet he practices that smile in the mirror." Who would know more about smile practicing than Sukie? His right cheek twitched when his smile was broadest. "That's a tell." Sukie had learned all about tells from him because he played poker and had taught the game to her and Mikey. A tell might be a scratch of the nose, a knuckle crack, a blink, perhaps even, yes, a twitch of the cheek—an unconscious giveaway that the player was bluffing, his hand of cards not a slam dunk but a great big nothing. Spot a tell and you spot a liar, her dad had told her. She noted that twitch when he got up from dinner before anyone had finished and, flashing his confident (or conman) grin, announced that he had to meet Mr. Black in Croton, and he'd be back late. His choice of names for his imaginary client, Mr. Black, indicated a dull mind. Sukie blamed her own lack of originality on her dad's genes.

"Black might invest in my building," said her dad.

Her mom poured herself another white wine and lifted her glass in a silent toast, more *adiós* than good luck.

"I doubt it," said Sukie.

"What?" said her dad.

Sukie turned to Señor at his usual place at the head of the table. "What do you think, Señor?"

Señor's eyes peered out under lids lowered to a lazy place between open and shut. He lapped his front teeth over his bottom lip, on one side only, a lopsided expression that Sukie had never seen before. The meaning was clear.

"He doesn't believe you," said Sukie.

"Weird," said Mikey, studying the dog. "He doesn't."

"Believe what?" said her mom.

"Good question." Her dad laughed. "I'll be back late. With a deal. I'll let the moon and the stars make my case."

He disappeared with a wave, and Sukie, with a sudden insight, flipped her fork off the table. Who buys a building in the dark? All that bunk about the moon and stars selling real estate. The sky was a cover, and he'd been using it for years. Sukie shivered at the thought. Years? Had this thing with the lady in Joe's Caffeinated been going on for years?

Mikey benefited from Sukie's distress, getting to ride in the front seat to school every morning while Sukie, in back, buried her head in a book. "Hey," her dad said now and then, "are you all right back there?" She knew he was trying to catch her eye in the rearview mirror.

"I'm studying." She kept her head down.

In AP algebra she got bored during a test, put down her pencil, and left half of the questions unanswered. "I got tired," she said when the teacher asked. On her way to US history, she dropped her penetrating analysis of Jeffersonian democracy in the trash can. She stopped doing all her homework, amazed at how her teachers swallowed her lies. "Mom's sick, I had to make dinner." "I had the stomach flu." "My computer crashed." Were they cutting her slack because she was the driven and studious Susannah Jamieson or because they thought her parents had fistfights?

Her experience of pretending to be dead on college night came in useful. In class she stopped participating, never even followed the action with her eyes. Mr. Vickers

snapped his fingers inches from her face. "What la
are you in? Come on, let's hear it. If you had to g
your daydream a country, what country would it be

"Hell," said Sukie.

The class laughed.

Sukie pulled a hair out.

Mr. Vickers removed his glasses and polished
lenses with his nubby sweater. "Yes, well, hell. Ne
been there myself. You'll present your *Madame Bo*
essay last," he told Sukie. "Hell sucks, and the
back takes forever, not to mention it's uphill. Have
finished your report?"

"Not really," said Sukie, who hadn't been plan
to do it at all.

Waving the book, he recited Flaubert's words f
memory. "'All the bitterness of life was served up to
on her plate.' What does that mean?"

"I hate my topic. Can I change it?" Ethan as
ignoring the question, which made Sukie war
scream. All the bitterness of life was served u
her plate. She knew what it meant. She was so r
smarter than everyone else.

During lunch, she sat alone at a corner table e
nothing and glowering. Across the room, Aut

size zero, lapped icing off a brownie as if she were making love to it. Watching her, Sukie's bond with Emma Bovary grew fiercer. I'm trapped in Tostes too, she thought, that puny village where nothing new ever happens. Flaubert is writing about me. She'd let her work in other classes slide, but she'd write this paper. In this single instance she'd enlighten her classmates. They deserved enlightening.

She didn't notice Frannie and Jenna, standing with their trays, observing. Frannie, unself-conscious when deep in thought, made her Frankenstein face, which involved chomping her lower teeth repeatedly into her upper lip. She and Jenna whispered, Jenna shrugged, and a minute later, Sukie was surprised by the plunk of their trays onto the table.

"Want to come with us on Saturday? Simon and me and Jenna and James?" said Frannie.

Sukie had heard that Frannie was hanging out with a guy named Simon, a senior at Poughkeepsie High.

"We're going in search of the red-tailed hawk," said Frannie. "There's been a sighting. It sounds awful but it will be fun."

Jenna held out a paper bag. "Have some biscotti. They're brilliant. James made them."

"I'm busy on Saturday," said Sukie, taking a biscotti. "And these seats are saved." It amused her to say that. *I'm busy. These seats are saved.* As if she were beating off friends with a stick.

Without a word Frannie and Jenna moved on.

Sukie ate the biscotti.

At night she quit playing *Jeopardy!* *Big deal, I know facts,* she wrote in her journal. *If you want a fact, Google it.*

In the mornings she dressed blind. She opened her drawer and put on the first thing her hand touched. She made a fetish of it, actually—of her refusal to care about what she wore—until it occurred to her that the first shirt might bring good luck. With that thought, she took the second shirt. Bad luck—bring it on, thought Sukie. I'm a festival of bad luck.

She left her phone at home. She'd lost interest in selfies. Completely.

Afternoons Sukie skipped tennis, canceled flute, ignored her homework. On the debate team, when she had to defend the statement "Glass ceilings exist," she stood up, did her special twist at the waist to appear ramrod straight, looked everyone dead in the eye as her father had counseled, and said, "Who gives a shit?"

She ditched tutoring.

Instead she went to the nearest Starbucks to get an espresso (which, for coffee, sounded tough), and bum a cigarette. She'd never smoked before, except once at camp, but this seemed as good a time as any to get started. There was no smoking allowed at Starbucks, something she'd forgotten.

Afternoons she wandered aimlessly around Hudson Glen. Although she rarely fantasized about Bobo now and hadn't for a few weeks, she found herself on the lookout for a particular car, probably an old Chevrolet, maybe a Ford, the minty-green color so rusted it might have been torched, a broken taillight, and a slash of blue on the passenger door. This was Kiefer's car, Bobo's friend. Maybe he and Bobo would be cruising in it. That moment at the party when Bobo had beckoned her over, wiggling his finger, the time he'd shoved his entourage aside to reward her brilliance, "You got that right" . . . these were nothing to hang hopes on. Still, they glowed in retrospect, flickers of promise and joy on the dark side of the moon.

One afternoon she stopped at Clementi's.

She stood shyly near the door. A slow time. There

were only a few tables taken, but she didn't immediately spot Isabella at the computer at the back of the bar because of her hair. It was red now, the color of a polished Delicious apple.

She waited. Issy wiggled, one of her signature moves, which seemed to position her breasts more satisfactorily. She pulled a BlackBerry out of her back pocket, checked it, and slipped it back in. She was wearing six different colors, seven if you counted her hair. Sukie especially loved the thick turquoise socks that she paired with high-top sneakers.

Finally heading to the front of the restaurant, Isabella stopped short when she saw Sukie.

"Hi," said Sukie.

Issy came up with a smile. "Hi. Is your dad with you?"

"No," said Sukie. "Don't worry about that."

"What?" said Issy.

"I was just . . . nothing. He's not here." Sukie chewed her thumb, something she hadn't done since she was five.

"Oh my God, these menus are a mess." Issy picked up a bunch lying about on the hostess counter and stacked them. "You look so pretty. Well, you always look pretty. And it's so nice to see you—you haven't been here in a while. How many are you?"

Sukie had no idea what she was talking about. "How many am I?"

"For pizza?"

"Just me. I'm not hungry."

"I'll buy you a Coke. Diet Coke, right? Will," she called to the bartender. "Diet Coke with double lemon for this darling person. You'll love double lemon." She guided Sukie to a booth, and when Sukie sat down, she slid in on the other side, chatting the whole time. "I'm over my eyeballs in work. Plus I'm taking improv. Do you know what that is? It's acting class but basically you improvise. It's hard. You have to be really brave. Like last week I was an assassin, but I did the cutest thing. I pretended my machine guns were made by different fashion designers and I couldn't make up my mind about which gun went best with my outfit."

"That's so cool," said Sukie, suddenly feeling she might be hungry after all. "Could I have a slice?"

"Sure." Isabella flagged a waitress. "One slice of a margherita, please. And rush it."

The waitress put down Sukie's drink, and Issy

peeled the paper off the straw and popped it in. "There you go." She pushed the drink over.

"I love your hair," said Sukie.

"What color is it today?" asked Issy.

Sukie laughed, surprised she still knew how. Wasn't that just like Issy, pretending not to know her own hair color? She always said the best things.

"How's school?" asked Issy.

"I don't know. Okay. Do you like my dad?"

"What?"

"I just wondered what you thought of him."

Issy looked deep into Sukie's eyes. Sukie could feel her searching for a way to understand the question.

"I mean," said Sukie, "do you think he's nice?"

"Of course," said Issy. "He's very nice when he comes in. Oh God, it's Mr. Pulaski." She waved at a portly gentleman struggling to get his raincoat off. She leaned across the table and whispered. "I have to pay attention to him because he gives the hugest tips." She slid out of the booth. "It's so nice to see you. Tell your dad hi and your mom and Mikey." She kissed her hand and placed it on Sukie's cheek before turning away to charm Mr. Pulaski.

When Sukie tried to pay, the waitress told her it

was all taken care of, and Isabella waved good-bye from across the room.

On Saturday night when her parents were out and Mikey had a sleepover at Tyler's, Sukie poured a juice glass of vodka and, holding her nose, drank it without stopping. "No big deal," she told Señor after the final gulp. A minute later her legs went wobbly, and shortly after that she got the sensation that her head was filled with helium and might float away. Curious about what she looked like, she tottered up the stairs and into the bathroom, stubbing her toe on the door. "Ow. Ow, ow, ow." She grabbed her foot and collapsed on the bathmat. "Kiss and make toe better," she ordered herself, and tried unsuccessfully to bring her foot to her lips. She offered the toe to Señor for kissing. He wanted nothing to do with it.

Sukie bunched up her lips so her teeth protruded rabbitlike and craned high enough to catch her reflection. She pulled the ends of her mouth nearly to her ears and pinched her eyes down, making monster faces, then rolled herself up in the bathmat and stuck her head up to see what that looked like too. "You're nuts," she said to her reflection or her reflection said to her, she wasn't sure which. "You are sick, demented, and ugly."

Her face distorted, lips growing to gargantuan size, cheeks puffing, eyes shrinking to peas. One earlobe grew so long, she could have jumped rope with it. Sukie viewed these grotesque developments curiously, as if they were happening to someone else.

"Issy," she called, but because her tongue felt thick, "Issy" came out "Ithy."

In the mirror, Isabella obligingly appeared, eating a slice. She sat on a chrome chair, the kind Sukie had seen at Joe's Caffeinated.

"No, please." Sukie struggled to enunciate. "Sit anywhere but in that chair."

Issy stood up and kicked the chair sideways, out of the reflection.

"Thanks," said Sukie.

"No problem," said Issy.

"My dad's slime, what am I going to do?" The words bumped into one another.

"Slime? I think he's charming."

"You do?"

"Absolutely. Want a slice?"

Sukie shook her head no.

Issy ripped off a piece of crust and crunched it. "It was fun to see you today."

"Same here," said Sukie.

"We really have to go shopping, little sister. You're fun."

"But my dad's slime." Big fat tears rolled down her engorged cheeks. She poked out her tongue, large as a giant lizard's, and swung it this way and that trying to lap up the tears. "Do you think Bobo will ever text me again?"

"It's possible," said Issy.

"Really?"

"Sure. But do you care?"

"I can't talk anymore. I don't feel good," said Sukie, and she threw up.

The next night, while her dad was watching football, Sukie backed quietly out of the living room and ducked into her dad's office. She could hear him cursing the ref—the Giants were losing—as she fumbled though the stuff on his desk. He always emptied his pockets next to his laptop after he came home from work: keys, money clip, change, BlackBerry, a credit card receipt or two. She wanted to check his calls and email. She wanted to know about the woman. But the BlackBerry wasn't there.

And it wasn't there the next night or the next,

but then on the way to school, her dad pulled into the Sunoco station for gas while talking business on his cell. He shut off the car, chatted a bit more, hung up, and dropped the BlackBerry on the seat.

While he strolled up to the pay window in his lazy, handsome-guy way, Sukie threw herself over the seat and snatched it.

"What are you doing?" said Mikey.

"Shut up or I'll tell everyone you masturbate." She scrolled through the numbers, glancing up every second or two. Her dad was charming the cashier. One number turned up a ton of times with no name attached: 666 555-7372. A rap on the window. Sukie jerked up. Her dad smiled and twirled his finger, meaning open the window.

Sukie lowered the glass, "You scared me. I forgot my phone, I was calling it for messages."

He put out his hand. She handed him his BlackBerry. 666 555-7372. 666 555-7372. Her dad winked at her through the windshield while he filled the tank. And Sukie, forcing a smile back, opened her spiral notebook. 666 555-7372. She scribbled it down.

As soon as she got to school, she ripped the number out of her notebook, folded it into a tiny wad, and tucked it in her wallet.

She was going to call the number. But she didn't. Every day or so she unfolded and read the number again, folded it up, and tucked it back inside her wallet.

Thanksgiving came and went. Sukie's family always celebrated with her aunt, who lived across the river in New Jersey. There were so many guests that no one noticed that Sukie barely spoke a word.

One evening, as her mom stood on her tiptoes trying to reach a champagne glass on a top shelf, and her father had phoned to say he wouldn't be home for dinner, Sukie nearly blurted, "Dad's cheating on you."

"Can you get that for me?" her mom asked. "I've got a craving for the bubbly."

"Sure, Mom." Sukie handed her the glass. *Dad's cheating on you.* She imagined the consequences. Her mother's grip would tighten in a spasm, the crystal would shatter, and the shards would rain down to reflect their brittle and broken world.

"I'm a little scared of champagne corks, aren't you?" Pointing the bottle toward the pantry, her mom closed her eyes. The cork shot out and hit a cabinet. Champagne spurted, and she caught the overflow in her glass. "It's really a man's job."

"What is?"

"Opening champagne." She took a sip and moaned in happiness. "Ooh, that's delicious. Do you think your dad's up to something?"

The question so shocked Sukie that for a second she thought she might have actually told her mom about her dad without realizing it. Or had her mom read her mind?

"His business is so peculiar," said her mom.

"He buys and sells real estate," said Sukie.

"I didn't mean his business business."

"What do you mean?"

"I like to think he has a secret life, that underneath all this perfection, things are more exciting. All this perfection." She raised her hand and fluttered her fingers.

Was her mom suspicious, amusing herself, simply being provocative, or assuming an attitude that went with champagne? Sometimes her mom accessorized a drink with a mood or vice versa. In the past Sukie had read visual clues. These days she was clueless.

In terms of swelling and bruising, her mom's face was nearly normal, but the result was less her mother than a mask of her mother. The skin stretched tight across her cheeks reminded Sukie of American cheese. In the way that American cheese, absolutely smooth and flat, didn't quite resemble cheese, her mother's skin didn't quite resemble skin. Processed, that's what it was, her mom's skin looked processed. As for her lips, they were more severe, as if someone had pulled and tacked them down. Even at rest they appeared to be heading toward some expression, but who knew what? The nose was still a mystery under a narrow strip of tape, but the eyes . . . here Sukie had spent considerable time figuring out what was different. An absence of friendly smile lines to be sure, but the change was less in the way her mother's eyes looked than in the way Sukie felt looking at them. Now a look at her mother turned into a search for her mother. Where was she in there? Might this feeling have to do with the fact that her mom's eyes were wide open, wide open every single second (apart from blinking) as if she were in a permanent state of surprise, or had the surgeon made some other minuscule adjustment that Sukie couldn't pinpoint? She imagined diving into her mom's eyes and splashing helplessly. "Mom, Mom, where are you?" The doctor stole her soul, thought Sukie, and gave it to someone else.

What a predicament. She couldn't bear to set eyes on her father, and when she set eyes on her mother, she couldn't find her.

Long into the night she labored on her English essay, and the next morning she dressed in head-to-toe black to present it. Before entering Mr. Vickers's class she took a selfie. She looked killer, a touch of lipstick and a pinch of each cheek, what Emma Bovary might do for a faint glow. She adopted a measured walk, each step discrete, intentional. No smiles, a simple slight narrowing of the lips indicating a private amusement of some sort that she would share with no one . . . yet.

"Our last day with Madame Bovary," Mr. Vickers announced. "No tears, please. Sukie, let's hear what you've written."

Sukie slid out of her chair, stood, and shifted her shoulders back, which had the side effect of lengthening her neck and giving her chin a bully's tilt. She took five steps to the front of the room and pivoted. "'Like Tostes, Like Cobweb,'" she said. "By Susannah Danielle Jamieson." Spinning Vickers's empty chair out from around his desk, she planted her black-booted foot on it.

The move was a shocker. Several classmates stopped

secretly texting. No one had ever taken possession of Vickers's chair and branded the seat with their boot.

She took a while to peruse the room, and then—thrilled with her topic sentence, it was perfection—drilled the words into the skulls of her classmates.

"Although we live more than a century and a half apart, although Emma Bovary is a fictional character and I'm real, although she's a French housewife and I'm an American high-school student, our lives could not be more similar.

"Every day in Tostes, a puny provincial town, Emma's life had the predictability of a metronome, those little mechanical devices that tick-tock tick-tock with screaming regularity. The schoolmaster opened the shutters of his house, the policeman passed, the horses crossed the road, the barber paced, her husband took hours nightly to eat smelly boiled meat.

"How could I not identify?

"Since kindergarten I've endured Ethan's relentless warnings of global warming, his hallelujah chorus of save the planet, his uniform"—she insulted that word, slathered it with sarcasm—"of cargo pants bulging with flyers, and his endless whining, 'Can I change my topic?' Yes. Change it and shut up!"

There was a burst of laughter.

Ethan's large round eyes blinked rapidly behind his glasses. He stopped proofreading a notice about a dire situation—algae in drinking water—and pushed out a smile. As he forced himself to meet the eyes of his classmates, his head jerked.

Sukie continued blandly. "Every day in the cafeteria, Autumn, the human wire hanger, performs brownie consumption. We see you. We get the message: 'Here's what I can eat and still poke your eye out with my elbow.' Your favorite actress is Cate Blanchett. 'She's so real.' Tell me that one more time and I'll scream. Does anyone here not know that Denicia has allergies? Has Denicia not brought up her allergy to cornmeal every single time she buys lunch? And how often is cornmeal on the menu? Never."

A wave of titters, but the laughter was more tentative, kids realizing, as Sukie trashed Autumn and then Denicia, that soon she would eviscerate *them*. And she did. Fleur for her mindless obsession with nails (an idiot savant, she called her, whose area of brilliance was manicures). "You either lose them or break them, is there any other choice? Perhaps you could choke on one."

Frannie was next.

Only here did Sukie waver. She skipped the sentence about how Frannie's mournful eyes raised themselves from doodling only to judge, and rushed on to Troy—sticking him for sneaking the Olympics and fencing into every single sentence. "Is Jenna a cheerleader?" she asked. "Yes, except the team she's jumping for is James. 'Isn't he wonderful?' Squeal, squeal, squeal. Congratulations, you have a boyfriend and can point your toe over your head. Whoopee."

Sukie's eyes danced from one student to the next, enjoying the possibility of increasing his or her discomfort. Troy had a smirk stuck on his face, Jenna's face flushed red, Fleur's teeth were bared—perhaps she would stab Sukie with her nail. Many students lowered their eyes or turned away. I'm an alpha dog—Sukie managed to squeeze in that pleasing thought while reading her essay. Her slightest glance produced submission, although not in Frannie, who had abandoned her drawing to rest her chin in her hands and regard Sukie frankly.

Sukie hit the principal for being "a crashing bore." The three C's were not creativity, community, and culture, but conformity, claustrophobia, and control. Showing off her critical prowess, Sukie managed to relate that to Flaubert's use of metaphor, and then, surging with power, she launched into her closing paragraph. "One test of a great book," she said, "is not whether it worked when it was written but whether it resonates across time. When I read that Emma, with her exquisite taste, had to endure the sight of her husband, Charles, in his dowdy clothes while I endure the daily vision of Mr. Vickers in his loud, baggy sweaters—that tells me that I've read a classic." Sukie then praised Flaubert for his prescience—exposing the stifling life at Cobweb 110 years before Cobweb existed—and concluded with a final condemnation: "Thanks to all of you, my soul suffocates. My spirit bleeds. Just like Emma's."

She removed her booted foot from the seat of Vickers's chair and returned to her seat.

Mr. Vickers crossed his arms, seized the bottom of his thick sweater with its colors as random as spin art, and, in one motion, pulled it over his head and off. Sukie expected that, underneath, he would be wearing a T-shirt. Who wears a big heavy sweater with nothing under it? Vickers, apparently. His pale hairless chest was muscled, his abs defined, his arms positively sculpted. Under that shapeless blob of yarn,

Vickers had a body, stocky but buff. From the class there were a few gasps, strangled snorts of laughter here and there, but mostly a hushed astonishment.

"If, by my taste in sweaters, I've contributed to your misery, please forgive me," he said.

Sukie nodded. If he expected her to wilt or apologize, the man could guess again. A hidden truth, she thought, observing his ripped bod. Vickers is hot. I've done him a favor.

He continued, rambling on about Flaubert as if he weren't half naked, as if tufts of hair weren't peeking from his underarms.

Sukie, meanwhile, sat primly, her ankles crossed, her hands clasped, aware in a satisfied way of everyone hating her.

"Oh, Sukie." Vickers summoned her when class was over and motioned that she should sit. She waited while he brushed the lapels of his sports jacket, which was always draped neatly over his chair, before he slipped it on over his naked torso.

"What's going on?" asked Vickers.

Sukie blew on her palm.

"I'm worried about you."

Sukie flipped her hand over and blew on the back

of it. Her first F. She was about to get her first F. What would it feel like? Cool.

"You upset your classmates. Why?"

"How'd you like my essay?"

Vickers took his time, loading his briefcase with papers. "It was original," he said finally. "Very original. But I'd expect a backlash. You can go now."

The Mirror

THANKS to the wonder of text messaging, some of which had taken place during class, Sukie's mockery of all kids and things Cobweb had spread through school before she even left the classroom. Kids were excited to hate her for a good reason rather than for her simply being arrogant or beautiful or clueless, or because her parents hit each other and consequently, inexplicably but nevertheless, that made her a freak. Excited to hate her, yes, though with some grudging respect and glee for her skewering Vickers on account of his nasty sweaters. Given the nature of text messaging—brief and therefore either to the point or misleading—many texts omitted exactly what or how much Vickers had taken off. Many kids believed he had stripped to his briefs.

Classmates fell back, repelled by her presence. She had an unobstructed path to the library and headed there in a daze. Original. Vickers had called her original. For once she wasn't practical, efficient, driven, organized, analytical, resourceful, or brilliant. She was original. She wanted to leap and jump and kick and scream, "I'm original!" For the meanest thing she'd ever done. *For the meanest thing I've ever done?* How confusing. Don't dwell on that part, she told herself, and didn't until something hit her in the face. Fleur had ripped off a nail and flicked it at her.

"I'm original." She burst into her house needing to tell someone. Louisa, the housekeeper, was cleaning the kitchen.

"The only reason I didn't tell your mother is she'll kill you," said Louisa before Sukie could say hello.

"Tell her what?"

Louisa shooed Sukie up the stairs. She was chubby but nimble.

"What is it, Louisa?" said Sukie.

"You tell me what it is." She grabbed Sukie's hand and pulled her through her bedroom to her bathroom. Mikey was sitting in the sink, his legs dangling in front of the cabinet below.

"It's not my fault he's in the sink. Get your butt out of my sink."

"I just cleaned that sink," said Louisa. "Get out, Mikey."

"No way," said Mikey.

"Why is he my fault?" asked Sukie.

"He's not. This is." She clamped her hands on Sukie's hips and spun her to the mirror.

"Uh-oh," said Sukie.

"I never would believe this if I didn't see it," said Louisa. "I've known you since you were five."

The mirror had splintered into a patchwork of cracks. Sukie's broken face stared back at her. A wicked diagonal slashed her mouth into a sneer, a vertical split bumped her nose into her left cheek and isolated her right cheek as if it were an island she might visit. Hairline cracks left her alluring eyes misshapen, one higher than the other, and her forehead as lined as Vince's, and he'd spent his life playing tennis in the sun. "Señor! Señor!" Sukie waved. "Come!"

"He never comes," said Mikey, which was true.

Sukie lugged him into the bathroom, all thirty-five pounds. "Señor." She showed him the mirror.

"What happened? Tell me."

He refused and appeared not remotely thrown by the broken reflection of his dangling hind legs, giving the impression that he had eight. "Tell me you've been screaming."

"The dog didn't do it. Get real," said Louisa.

Sukie knew she was right.

"Such a beautiful mirror. Think of the things it's seen, and now look what you've done to it."

"Me? I didn't do this. It's old. It's cracking up."

"You're lucky I don't tell your mother anything," said Louisa. And she left.

Sukie swayed, watching her reflection warp in new and more tortured ways. Had she done it? Was that possible?

"When are you going back to the club?" said Mikey.

"I've given up tennis. Leave me alone."

"If you don't go, I can't. Dad doesn't go anymore."

"Probably because of the grim man." Tears welled in her eyes, mercifully and briefly blurring her reflection. "I'm original," she whispered to the mirror. Yes, but in an ugly way, it seemed to say back.

"Please go to the club," said Mikey.

"You just want to see Marie's boobs."

"Please."

"No."

"If you don't go to the club, I'll tell Mom about the mirror. How you busted it." With a boost from his hands he sprang from the sink, took two steps toward the door, which put his sister in striking distance, and bolted past.

Dad and Mom

HER mother alive yet fixed in time, as if someone had hit the pause button. Her mother at the window. From the back. Arms stiff by her side, hair immaculate as always, chopped blunt, and able to swing, every hair in unison, considered an achievement but merely genetic good fortune. But no movement now. Her long neck pale, innocent, exposed. A blouse of silk as light and soft as rose petals.

"I'm going to teach you to cry on command."

The voice didn't come from her mother but from somewhere else.

Out the long and narrow window—body length like Sukie's mirror—out the window, water. Was the window a window or was it a glass? Or was it a bottle? A bottle of what? What a view. Of water, halfway up the window, lapping the pane. Water as clear and empty as bathwater, and above it a sky of endless blue. No sign of life, no horizon even—how was that possible? Except for, bobbing in the distance, a speck of white. Floating closer. A paper folded in half, in quarters, yet again. A tiny wad. As her mom reached for it, Sukie reached and touched her shoulder. "Mom."

Her mother turned.

Not her mother, lifelike but not alive. Eyes as vacant as a doll's. Cheeks as smooth as china, a painted mouth. A hole in the center. A puncture for a nose. "Mom! Mom!" The window splintered. "The mirror cracked," screamed Sukie. And the water rushed in.

Sukie's eyes opened, her heart pounded, her body pulsed with electricity. The jumps, a full-blown attack. A terrible dream. "Señor?" Where was his comforting body? The door of her dark bedroom opened.

Her dad tripped over Señor and belly flopped onto the floor.

Sukie vaulted out of bed. "Señor! Señor! Are you all right?"

Her father, sprawled across the carpet, took a while to organize—pull his arms in, tuck his legs under, and sit up.

"Did he hurt you? Did he?" Sukie cooed in Señor's ear.

"To hell with the dog. What about me?" Her dad grabbed the edge of the bed and, with a groan, hoisted himself to standing. Upright, he rocked unsteadily.

Sukie continued to fuss over Señor.

"He's fine," said her dad. "What was he doing there?"

She wondered. Usually he slept next to her, squeezing her into a sliver of space between him and the wall. On rare occasions, lightning storms, he migrated around the room. There was no storm tonight, and was it by chance that he had lain in that spot by the door, on his tummy with his hind legs extending straight behind him and his front paws reaching forward (his most human pose, kind of a dead-man's float or, considered differently, the way a child might lie while playing with Hot Wheels)? Measured in feet, his longest position, a substantial barrier. Her dad coming into the room would inevitably trip and crash.

"I've missed my daughter," he said.

"I was asleep. It's two in the morning."

He pressed his palms against his head, removed them, and waited before speaking, waiting, it seemed, to see if his head might fall off. "Where have you been?"

"What are you talking about?"

"I don't know. How's that quarterback, you still dating him?"

"If I want."

"Way to go."

Sukie got up. "Dad, I'm really tired."

"Gotcha."

He looked over at the wall, at his own shadow, looming large. Sukie took it in too. A monster in moonlight. "Your mom drinks more than me," he said. "Come on, admit it."

"Sure," said Sukie.

He took an exaggerated step over Señor. Sukie slid back under the covers.

"I thought you were supposed to reject your *mother.*"

"What?" said Sukie.

"You know, girls." He pulled the door closed behind him.

Morning distressing, Sukie wrote in her journal. *Hard to keep head up. Couldn't sleep for hours after Dad woke me. Drunk? Maybe. Regarding my mirror. Trying to figure it out. Trying to push it out of my brain. Both things. Too upsetting. Could it be my fault? Is that possible? I researched telekinesis, psychokinesis (essentially the same thing), and paranormal happenings. There is no scientific evidence that these phenomena exist, only tales and stories, which means the answer is no.*

"Soo-kie." Mikey smacked open her door. "Five minutes starting now or I tell Mom. No, four."

Mikey in my face. God. Sukie slammed her journal shut, went down to the kitchen, and while she shook some granola into a bowl and Mikey watched, dialed Vince's number.

"Where have you been?" he barked at her. "I heard you quit the team. Why did you do that?"

"I don't know," said Sukie, pouring in soy milk.

"I believe that," said Vince.

"Can I come for a lesson on Sunday?"

"You bet. See you at ten, missy, and bring your head."

"There. Satisfied?" she said to Mikey, who leaped his way out of the kitchen.

Suppose I see the grim man? She stood at the counter, pressing soggy granola bits down into the milk and watching them float up again. *Suppose he's at the club? What do I do?*

In the dining room, her mother upended a shopping bag. Bottles of nail polish clattered onto the lacquer table. "Whoops." She corralled them before they spun off. A ray of sunlight so blinding it could trick a person into believing it was warm outside on a freezing winter day made Sukie move slightly left to confirm that her mom's face was finally done. The stitches in her ripped earlobe had come off last week, and now the last little piece of tape, the one across her mother's nose, was off as well.

She came up quietly as if stalking prey. "Your nose," said Sukie.

"The doctor said I could take the tape off. Like it?"

"It's great," said Sukie, which was the only acceptable answer.

Technically her mother's nose was "ski slope," but for the first time Sukie realized the inadequacy of those web classifications. Yes, her mom had had her "ramp" eradicated, and in its place the doctor had sculpted a narrow scooped protuberance. Protuberance. In the future that's what she'd call it, a protuberance, as if her mother's new nose were not even a nose but a site. Something one might view like a bridge or a monument or a curious mound. But while technically it was "ski slope," in reality its label should be "gone."

Because without realizing it, Sukie had pinned her hopes on that taped protuberance. When it was finally revealed, she would find that her mother had preserved the one thing they had in common. Their bond. "I couldn't bear to change my nose," her mother would say.

Somehow all these changes—the cheeks as smooth as cheese, the permanently stretched mouth, the empty eyes—all these perfectly beautiful elements that didn't belong together and would always lack the wonderful interactive mobility that make features a face . . . none of them would matter if Sukie and her mom still had the same nose. They would still "go together."

Now that dream was dead. It had been, Sukie realized, a delusion. In its place was her nightmare. Her mother was gone.

The Club

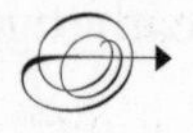

MIKEY'S mad dash out of their mom's car to hang out with Marie didn't blunt Sukie's terror of having to return to the club, but she did feel that she was suffering for a good cause. She'd given him a gift. This lone act of generosity in her self-obsessed life provided a glimmer of hope that she wasn't one hundred percent hateful.

She entered surreptitiously.

Back to the wall, she jutted her head for a sneak peek into the clubhouse foyer. No grim man.

She scooted past the tabletop Christmas tree decorated as it was every year with shiny oversized red bulbs, halted to peep into the bar, where Mikey was already spinning on a stool while Marie set him up with a Coke. No grim man there, either, only a table of folks drinking Bloody Marys. Sukie sprinted past, threw a look over her shoulder to see if the grim man might be trailing her, and then approached the card room, where, despite its being only ten in the morning, poker was already happening. The clatter of chips. The electricity of men and women involved in a game of deceit, strategy, and money. Poker is training for life, her dad had told her. Even if the grim man were there, and she didn't check thoroughly, he would be too absorbed to spot her.

She sped by and into the café.

She'd always loved this spacious room, peaceful and subdued, with walls of glass offering a view onto the parklike grounds, the round tables spaced far apart, the wicker armchairs so large that diners were barely visible. Sukie had lunched here with her parents every Sunday back when her parents enjoyed each other. When was that? She tried to remember. Mikey was in a booster seat then. Her mom picked at a chicken salad, her dad dove into a steak, and Sukie and Mikey ordered from the kids' menu, grilled cheese and chips. Sometimes they played I Spy or Twenty Questions. Today she walked through quickly, holding up her racket so the crosshatching of strings obscured her face.

Once she was outdoors where the courts were, a sense of contentment washed over her. Even in the dreary onset of winter, with the clipped hedges bare and the grass dry and stubby, the order and geometry soothed.

A thermometer hanging from a lamppost read forty-five degrees. Only die-hard players, a group that used to include Sukie and her dad, turned out in early December, rubbing their hands together, blowing into them for warmth before seizing their rackets and jogging onto the court. Rain, ice, or snow might keep them away, but a sharp wind that made it necessary to toss up a service ball several times before it didn't arc out of reach was a challenge they welcomed, proof even of character.

Sukie broke into a run down the path and onto the court. She stripped off her winter gloves. When she was six years old and her dad had first put a racket in her hand, he'd showed her how to grip it like a firm handshake. She felt the same shiver, of an adventure about to begin, as she slipped her hand around the taped racket handle and held it tight.

How happy she was to see Vince. Bandy-legged and stiff, although improbably quick when playing, he ambled like a cowpoke as he picked up stray balls from his last lesson. He hadn't changed—not that she expected his face to be "under construction" or anything like that, and it had been only a couple of months since she'd last seen him—but his dependable ignorance of fashion cheered her. There he was as usual in his faded sweatshirt so shrunk that when he raised his racket to wave, a bit of his potbelly showed.

He bounced a ball and hit it over.

Sukie pivoted, took a step, bending her knee deeply, and sent back a topspin forehand that nipped the line.

With that one shot, the pleasure of single focus and the game of tennis consumed her. One thing mattered: getting her shots right. She forgot her dad, the woman with the wavy black hair, the grim man, her mom and how lonely she felt whenever she saw her. *Keep your eye on the ball. Keep your eye on the ball.* Vince's refrain was a mantra. Soon she had peeled off her hoodie and sweat pants and was down to a T-shirt and shorts. Her flushed face glistened with sweat.

There was a moment when she chased down a ball and found herself at the sideline facing the court where her dad had played. The court was empty, and for a brief time she recalled her dreamy state, looking without seeing into the sparklingly clear day until the man in the red Windbreaker had punched her dad. One, two. A one-two punch and her dad had toppled as if he weighed nothing at all.

"Missy," Vince called.

She trotted back to the baseline, and when she slammed the next backhand, a noise burst from her. Loud, guttural, somewhere between a grunt and a roar. Again and again, shot after shot she exploded with these uninhibited, unladylike, grunty, piglike bursts of passion.

"About that marshmallow in your brain," said Vince when the lesson was over. He poked a finger into her forehead. "I didn't see it today. Today I saw a warrior. It's too late now, missy, but get back on the team in the spring."

"I will," said Sukie. "Thanks for the lesson. I missed tennis."

Elated, she ran off the court. In the nearly deserted club grounds, she halted, arched back, spread her arms as if she were greeting the sky, and spun.

She sprinted and, like a hurdler, leaped one hedge, then another, landed with a thump, and stumbled, which only made her laugh. Someone caught her arm to help her up.

"Are you all right?" he asked.

Even before she heard his voice, she recognized his grip, his rough strong grasp, his thumb pressing her biceps, and something else she hadn't remembered before but recognized now, a chrome watch with an accordion band. Up she jerked and saw the thin lips, the eyes deep set under a wide forehead. Looking into his eyes was like looking into a canyon. His voice, mellow with concern, shocked her. She'd expected menace. So there was a disconnect—it was the grim man and it wasn't. He was young, boyish, that was something else she hadn't realized. How old was he? She guessed about thirty. Her dad was forty-five. That made what he'd done even crueler, beating up an older man.

"Are you all right?" he asked again.

Sukie nodded.

"Good." He smiled, which was loathsome. How dare he smile at her? And then he moved right along, resuming his conversation with his friend. She had been a brief charitable stop on the road. He didn't remember her. He didn't even remember her hair.

The grim man had passed three courts and was nearly at the locker room when Sukie ran after him. "Excuse me," she called. "Excuse me, excuse me."

He swung around. "What is it, sweetheart?"

Sweetheart? That impertinence nearly knocked the thoughts out of her head. "I'm Sukie," she said, and when he didn't react, added, "I'm Warren Jamieson's daughter."

He turned to his friend. "You go on. I'll catch you later."

His friend disappeared into the locker room. The grim man waited for the door to slowly click shut.

"I scared you that day, right? I'm sorry." He unwrapped a stick of gum and folded it into his mouth. "Want a piece?" he asked, almost as an afterthought.

"No," said Sukie with horror.

His jaw moved around. Sukie suspected he was

suppressing a smile, but perhaps he was simply chewing.

"Why did you punch my dad?"

"Ask him."

And he was gone. Into the men's locker room. She couldn't follow even if she'd wanted.

Home

WAITING outside the club with Mikey, Sukie slid the tiny wadded paper from her wallet and tucked the wallet back into her tote. *Ask your dad. Ask your dad.* Unable to unfold it with gloved hands, she tugged finger by finger with her teeth and let the gloves fall to the ground. Then she opened and flattened the scrap, smoothing it on her palm. 666 555-7372. The number was barely decipherable, a rushed scrawl right after her dad had rapped on the car window and put out his hand for his BlackBerry.

Her memory of Joe's Caffeinated was getting fuzzy. Sometimes she imagined it wasn't her father. She'd barely seen the man, after all. Although he did ask for water as only her dad did, but perhaps that was a coincidence. "A glass of tap." Did anyone else say that? Could it be common slang in Minneapolis, where he grew up? Sometimes she tried to construct another explanation for what she'd witnessed, but with her dad's arm around the woman and their hands tangling, untangling, she always came to the same conclusion. Betrayal, not friendship. She was sure the grim man had something to do with this. "It's just business," her dad had told her. But was it? *Ask your dad. Ask your dad.*

Mikey snatched the scrap of paper and ran off.

"Mikey!" She chased and tackled him. They hit the hard ground. She held him down, pried open his fist, and got the paper back.

Sukie rolled sideways, unpinning him. "Why did you do that?"

"I felt like it."

"Jerk."

She grabbed her tote and tennis racket, which she'd dropped, stuck the paper back in her wallet, scooped up her gloves, and flopped down next to her brother. He was eating.

"What have you got?"

"Peanuts. From Marie. They don't have pretzel

sticks anymore." He offered the baggie full.

They sat there munching, waiting for their mom or dad to show up.

"I hate Mom's face," said Sukie.

"It's better if you watch her teeth," said Mikey. "Her teeth are the same. I watch her teeth."

With her tote for a pillow, Sukie relaxed back, enjoying the parade of broken clouds drifting across a pale December sky, the sun appearing and disappearing, cutting through the chill to warm her face, then leaving her in shadow again.

"The trees are singing," said Mikey.

And Sukie, resting, heard the wheezing tune of a breeze strumming the bare branches of an oak.

A car horn interrupted her good feelings. She bounced up expecting to see the Bronco. Instead there was Heather's little yellow Volkswagen. Heather, Mikey's occasional sitter, leaned across the front seat and yelled out the window, "Hey, you guys.

"Sunroof or no sunroof?" she asked when they got in.

"Sunroof," said Mikey.

"How come you're here?" asked Sukie.

"Search me. Your mom called and said she couldn't

pick you up." Heather turned up the volume on her CD player. The Dave Matthews Band blared, and she forced them to listen to a saxophone solo over and over all the way home.

Weird, thought Sukie, as they walked up the path to the front door. Very weird. Both cars are in the driveway. A sudden shiver of trepidation. "Let's go in the back," she was telling Mikey when her dad flung the front door open and stopped short at the sight of them.

His face was pale and strained. Every feature pulled toward the center. The up energy that propelled him through the day, that take-charge thing he'd even mustered on the tennis court after he'd been slugged, was absent.

"I'm leaving," he said, and passed them right by.

Sukie took her brother's hand. Together they crossed the threshold. Upstairs on the landing Señor watched between the balustrades.

If I can get there, if I can just get Mikey and me to Señor, it will be all right, Sukie thought. The marble foyer seemed huge, a flat plain with no protection. They were walking targets. "Walking targets"—that's how she thought of herself, how scared she was that she might find herself in the crosshairs of her mother's rage.

They reached the stairs and were about to rush up. "I need to talk to you, Sukie," her mom called, and when Sukie didn't turn or reply, issued a more demanding, "Sukie, I need you."

"I didn't tell about the mirror," whispered Mikey.

"It's not about that." Sukie knew instinctively that it was about something else. She didn't know what, but something worse.

Slowly they approached the living room.

At first Sukie glimpsed a fragment, her mother's slippered feet propped up on the coffee table. As she came closer and the angle through the doorway widened, she got the whole picture—her mother slumped on the couch, a pillow clamped against her stomach, a fat wad of tissues clutched in her hand.

Her mother didn't turn her head to greet them. She gazed toward the window. "Go upstairs, Mikey." Her voice, hollow and wrung out, flattened to a monotone. "Take the dog with you."

"What dog?" The second Sukie said it, she realized that Señor had silently scooted down the stairs to her side.

"That dog makes me nervous, and God knows I'm already a wreck. Go on, take him, Mikey."

"How do I do that?" he asked. "Señor does whatever he wants. It's not like he's a remote control. I can't fix him." Mikey started crying for what seemed like no reason whatsoever. Sukie knew he was frightened.

"Señor, go upstairs with Mikey," Sukie whispered. "Please."

It was undoubtedly the "please" that did it. Please was essential with Señor. He led Mikey out.

"I should have realized when I saw the receipt." Her mom dabbed at her eyes with a tissue.

"The receipt?"

"But I was so worried about you and college. I wasn't thinking of myself. You didn't order a DVD, did you?"

"What are you talking about?"

"*The Other Boleyn Girl*. The receipt was in the glove compartment."

"I never saw that movie," said Sukie.

"Of course you didn't." Her mother slapped the throw pillow aside and straightened up. "All those mysterious nights out. Sit down."

The second Sukie did, her mom stood and began

pacing. Every so often her shoulders jerked or her elbows flapped or her side twitched. Big scarlet blotches of agitation spotted her face, which was otherwise drained of color.

"Where was Dad going?" asked Sukie.

"Your dad? You're worried about him?"

"No."

"I kicked him out."

"What?"

"I heard from Mrs. Dintenfass today."

"Mrs. Dintenfass?"

Her mother always did this. She fired a ball at Sukie and, before Sukie could catch it, pitched another. Her dad was kicked out? At the same time, Sukie scrambled to recall what she'd told Mrs. Dintenfass about her mother's facelift, about her dad being hit on the tennis court—yes, she'd told and sworn her to secrecy.

"Apparently when a student is doing as badly as you are, Mrs. Dintenfass telephones on Sunday. You're flunking everything. Except AP English, although you did something in that class, frankly I was so upset I couldn't follow exactly, but as a result, at school, you're a leper."

"She called just because I'm flunking?"

"Just?"

Sukie bit her lip.

"What about college?" Her mom's elbows flapped wildly. At any moment she would take off and crash through the picture window.

"It's not that big a deal."

"What's this?" said her mom.

Sukie walked over for a close look. A pile of Sukie's hair drifted like tumbleweed across the coffee table as her mom's flapping blew it sideways. "I found this in your drawer. Are you pulling out your hair?"

Sukie reached into her pocket and dumped on a fistful more. "As long as you're collecting."

Her mom blew her nose loudly, left the room, and returned with fresh tissues. "Oh, God, I need ginger, my stomach's all upset." She pivoted and left again. Sukie heard cabinets bang in the kitchen. Her mom returned, ripping the paper off some ginger taffy. She gnawed off a piece. For a while she simply chewed, which, with ginger taffy, was an effort.

"What were you doing in my drawer?" asked Sukie.

"You are way too smart to be flunking."

Was that an explanation? Her mom had a brain

like a maze: Try to follow the logic and you slammed into a dead end. "Why were you in my drawer?" she asked again.

"I was in your drawer because I was looking for your journal."

Sukie had never told her mother about her journal. "How did you know about my journal?"

"I'm a snoop. You have to be when you have kids, you'll see. I'm a snoop. Although I managed to miss something right under my nose."

"How dare you go in my journal? It's private."

"Not if you're on drugs."

"I'm not on drugs."

"How did I know that? If you're getting F's, what other explanation could there be?"

Her mom sat back down on the couch and drummed her fingers into her arms. "Thanks to you, I kicked your father out. Imagine how awful it was for me to be reading your journal, expecting to find out that my daughter's on speed or something, and find out instead . . ." She started quietly weeping, letting the tears flow, too defeated to raise a hand to wipe an eye. Sukie put her arm around her mother, who buried her head in Sukie's shoulder.

"I'm sorry, Mom."

Her mother's shoulders trembled as she sniffled and sobbed. She felt so frail. For Sukie it was like cuddling a bird.

Finally her mom raised her head, brushed her hair out of her eyes, and said, "You knew it all along."

"Sort of. Not really." Sukie's hand itched to grab some hair and yank, but she restrained herself. "I didn't know."

"It was in your journal. He didn't deny it."

"What did he say?" said Sukie.

"Nothing. Not a damn thing."

"So he didn't admit it?"

Her mother shrugged.

"Why did you steal a duvet?"

Her mother pushed her away. "What?"

On her life Sukie had no idea why she'd brought that up. If she could have sucked the words back into her mouth, she would have.

"Your dad told you that?" her mom demanded.

"Are you getting divorced?" asked Sukie.

"What a bastard he is. Get out." She flung an arm toward the hall.

Clueless about why she needed to do this but

nevertheless compelled, Sukie scooped up the pile of her old hair, all those golden strands she'd extracted, mementoes of hysteria past, and carried them out of the living room and up the stairs fast, then faster and faster.

"I wasn't stealing," her mom shouted. "I knew he'd pay for it."

Sukie tore around the landing and into her room. She slammed the door, dumped the hair on her desk, and threw herself on the bed. Her dad was leaving. Her dad whom she hated. Her dad who she wished were with her right here, right now. Her dad was abandoning her to her mom. Dad!

The door banged open.

Sukie flipped over.

Her mom, as rigid as steel, her hands clenched so tightly that her knuckles were white, hissed from the doorway. "I'm not surprised you don't have friends, the way you talk."

"What?"

"I want you out of this house. You're on his side. You've known about this. You kept me in the dark."

Sukie scooted back on the bed as her mother came toward her.

"Up. Come on, up and out. You kept the secret. Who is it?"

"I don't know," said Sukie.

"Funny, I always thought he was up to something. But I thought it was something exotic—guns to rebels."

"Guns to—? What rebels?" Her mom had shifted to an imaginary drama in the midst of a real one.

"All his charm." She slapped Sukie's face. "Who?"

"I don't know." Sukie rubbed her cheek.

"Well, you're out too." She yanked the spread, rolling Sukie off the bed.

Sukie raced out of the bedroom, her mom chasing behind.

"I hate you. I'll hate you forever," screamed Sukie.

"Don't forget a jacket. It's cold out," her mother said coolly from the top of the stairs. And Sukie, following one last piece of maternal advice, grabbed her parka off a hook before throwing open the front door and running out.

Frannie

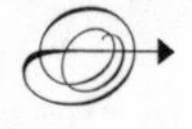

LOCUST Park banked steeply down toward the Hudson River. Depending on one's point of view, it was either amiably untended or wildly overgrown. The ancient locust trees, for which it was named, stripped of their foliage, revealed webs of spidery branches as intricate as snowflakes. Sukie never ventured here except when forced, like on school outings to study plants or bugs. Locust Park reminded her of the scary parts of animated movies where trees came alive, their branches snatching at a fair maiden running for her life. The maiden always had waves of golden hair like Sukie, and in one movie, the more she clawed to escape, the more entangled she became. Sukie still had nightmares about it.

She'd left the house in a burst of rocket fire, running for blocks. When she finally burned out, she found herself near the park. Rather than run away from this place that had always frightened her, she ran into it, an action that can be explained only by madness, the way someone being chased might select a dark alley over a busy thoroughfare.

She descended the narrow and uneven brick steps and then wended her way through the empty woods to one of the few park benches. Its slats were splintered. Only a few chips of brown indicated that it had ever been painted. It was now driftwood gray.

She couldn't say how long she sat there. She couldn't wrap her brain around a single coherent thought. She had no one to call. She had no friends. The deep loneliness of being friendless weighed on her. Why had she read that essay in Mr. Vickers's class? Why had she written it? She couldn't remember.

She hated her mother. Her mother was right to throw her out. These miseries reigned side by side. It wasn't that she had done anything wrong, she hadn't. It wasn't her fault about her dad. Nonetheless, she was a terrible person. This fate was something she deserved. As the sun dipped lower, she wondered if she would die from the elements and if everyone at Cobweb would cheer. She wasn't even sure what that meant, the elements. She dug her hands deep into her pockets and hunched against the cold.

She studied a little red scrap hanging high in a tree. An old balloon, she figured, captured, punctured, dead. Maybe it had suffered endlessly, losing air in little spurts day after day after day. Done in by the elements.

"Help!" A girl's voice giggled, and coming up the embankment, squealing about how she was going to fall any second, was Frannie. She was being pulled. A big hunk of a guy hauled her with both hands.

Frannie appeared momentarily stunned by the sight of Sukie, her lips and cheeks blue from cold, sitting stone still on a bench alone in Locust Park.

"Hi," said Frannie.

"Hello." Sukie forced naturalness into her voice.

"This is Simon. Simon Podansky, Sukie Jamieson."

"Yo." Simon stuck out a meaty hand to shake. He was nearly as tall as Sukie's dad and as sturdy as a ship you could sail into rough seas.

"We were watching the light," said Frannie.

"Oh," said Sukie.

Simon ran his hand over his wheaty white hair buzzed nearly to his scalp. "The sky pales, the winter sun burns cool," he said.

Sukie nodded, having no idea what he was talking about.

"Well, see you," said Frannie. "Aren't there steps around here?"

Sukie pointed in the direction she'd come.

"Thanks."

They hiked on. Sukie pulled her gloved hands out of her pockets and interlaced her fingers. *This is the church*—she raised her index fingers—*this is the steeple.* She stopped the children's game, remembering her dad's hand tangling, untangling, and the lady with the black wavy hair.

"Hey, Sukie-Lukie," Simon shouted. "Want a ride?"

"I like the bumper sticker," said Sukie, not because she did but because the sticker, MARRY ME AND BE MY CANOE, on Simon's old Toyota was unavoidably strange.

"Frannie made it for me. Where can I drop you?"

"You made it?" said Sukie, ignoring his question.

"When I first met him, he shouted, 'Marry me and

be my canoe.' It was so dumb. Also he ate art."

"What?" said Sukie.

"Not art, a leaf," said Simon.

"Art," said Frannie.

They both started laughing. Sukie couldn't make heads or tails of it, and not just because she was tired and sad. This was definitely a conversation a couple has that only they understand. That was the pleasure of it.

"So where do you want to go?" asked Simon.

"Clementi's," said Sukie, thinking of Issy. *If I had a little sister, I'd want her to be you*—that's what Issy had said. Could she crash at Issy's place? Suppose that boyfriend Richie was back? Suppose, well, anything, it was her day off or she didn't have room? Sukie took out her cell and scrolled as if she were considering the possibilities and there were so many.

"Come to my house," said Frannie.

"I'm not sure—"

"Simon's dropping me. He's got to write a paper. He still has school tomorrow. His school's not out for the holidays yet. Come on."

While Sukie and Frannie had never been friends, they'd known each other since the first grade. The last time Sukie had been to Frannie's was four years ago, for Frannie's eleventh birthday. In those days, when they were kids, when you gave a party, you invited everyone in your class and everyone came. Eleven was also the year of Sukie's last birthday party. To avoid the embarrassment of no one showing up, she pretended to her parents that there were more adult things she'd rather do, like see a play in New York City.

Frannie's place hadn't changed: a plain box of a house—wooden, two stories—painted a wintry blue and mostly hidden by a giant evergreen. Nothing fancy like Sukie's brand-new salmon-colored stucco house, no curved driveway or glamorous stained glass windows bordering an oversize front door.

As Sukie walked up the narrow brick path, she heard Frannie behind her whisper, "Isn't she beautiful?" Sukie strained to hear his reply.

"Plant one," said Simon.

Plant one? Sukie had never heard that expression, and she swiveled slightly to see Frannie throw her arms around him. They locked lips in a tender way, not hard and rough but hot. By "plant one," Sukie knew what he was saying: She may be beautiful but I'm interested only in you. Perhaps he was even saying that Frannie was beautiful, although strictly speaking, and Sukie was not being judgmental but simply accurate, Frannie was more interesting-looking than beautiful.

"Is he your boyfriend?" Sukie asked as he drove off.

"I don't use that word." Frannie grinned. "Do you think he's cool?"

"Well . . . ," said Sukie.

"He's not. He's not the least bit cool. I don't know what he is." She shrugged helplessly. "But he's something."

"I'm dating this smoldering guy, Bobo Deeb," said Sukie.

"Oh, yeah," said Frannie. "You mentioned him. The guy from Hudson Glen High. Hey, Mom," she shouted, opening the door.

In two shakes Sukie was swept into life in the Cavanaugh home. Frannie's mom and Mel, her step-dad, were in the kitchen making minestrone. Sukie was given a can opener and some jumbo cans of tomatoes, and then instructed to pour the tomatoes into a bowl and break them up with her hands. She didn't need to talk, a relief, except to answer that her parents were fine.

There was a plate of large green pellets, which Frannie's mom said were stuffed grape leaves. Sukie refused them even though she was starved because they looked weird, and stuck instead to the salted nuts and olives. Frannie's stepdad was talking about the Middle Ages and how people threw their leftovers to the dogs after they were done eating.

"I didn't know that," said Sukie. "What countries are you talking about exactly?"

"Are you interested in history?" he asked.

"I love history," said Sukie, and Mel was off and running about lute music in twelfth-century France. It turned out that he was a professor of history and writing a paper on it.

Sukie had never hung out anyplace where people talked about anything that had happened before last week. Frannie's mom, who owned a flower shop, had a few twigs in her hair that Mel plucked out. "You brought home souvenirs from the shop," he said.

"Things are very bad there, *monsieur*," said Frannie's mom. They burst out laughing.

"Oh, God," said Frannie. "Let's get out of here."

"It's a line from *Casablanca*," her mom explained. "It's an old movie, and in a scene where Rick tells a poor sad refugee to go back to Bulgaria, she says, 'Things are very bad there, *monsieur.*' We try to stick the line into as many conversations as possible."

"They're crazy," said Frannie.

"We are," said her mom. "Aren't we, Booper?" Apparently Booper was Mel's nickname.

Frannie dragged Sukie upstairs.

The walls of Frannie's bedroom were papered with art posters. "I'm currently into Dalí and Duchamp," she said, neither of whom Sukie had ever heard of. "In my own art, I've entered a bizarre period." There were a few pencil drawings of hers tacked up: a fish driving a car, a book with worms growing out of it, a bleeding wristwatch. Sukie studied them, feeling that she ought to know what to say but didn't.

A bunch of odd objects were displayed on a bookshelf: a doll leg, an old phone with a rotary dial, some bits of pottery, a bent silver fork. "What are these?" asked Sukie.

"Take away use and you have art," said Frannie. "That's what my dad always said. He saved all these things."

"Everything in my house is new," said Sukie. "Even my mother's face. She had it lifted."

"Oh, wow," said Frannie. "That explains it."

"We used to have the same nose, but not anymore."

"How weird." Frannie picked up the china-doll leg. It was as pale as marble with pink dimples painted on the knee. Its shoe was in perfect condition: red leather with a strap over a white cotton ankle sock. "Put out your palm."

Sukie opened her hand and Frannie laid the doll leg on it.

There was something compelling about it. It didn't seem broken, it seemed complete, and then it seemed shocking, evidence of an unknown unspeakable horror. Sukie shivered.

"Yeah," said Frannie. "I know. It's got this fabulous creepiness."

Frannie's face—long and solemn with big, dark brown, expressive eyes—was unpredictable. Sukie had always found that from one minute to the next you could think she was mocking you or being the friendliest. Although Frannie couldn't stop showing her dimples around Simon, usually she was slow to smile. Sometimes her eyes ached with pain. When that happened Sukie guessed that Frannie was thinking about her dad. Her parents had been divorced. Frannie had stopped by to visit her dad after school. It was she who found him dead. That made Sukie feel especially awful that she'd never said, "I'm sorry about your dad," and let the whole thing slide right by as if the tragedy in Frannie's life had never happened.

Right now Frannie was looking at Sukie so sympathetically that Sukie thought she had X-ray vision right to her heart.

Sukie carefully placed the doll leg back on the shelf. "Take away use and you have art. How cool," she said. "My mom kicked me out."

Frannie's door slammed open and Jenna burst in. When she saw Sukie, she went white. Her chin jutted forward, her face tightened into a fist.

"I can leave," said Sukie to Frannie.

"But you're sleeping over," said Frannie.

"I am?" said Sukie.

"She is?" said Jenna. "Maybe I'll leave."

"Please don't," said Sukie. "Please. I shouldn't have written that stuff about you. Or about anyone."

Jenna perched on the bed and let her purse hang between her legs. "Why did you?"

Sukie threw up her hands and, when she couldn't think of any words to go with that helpless gesture, clamped her head as if to stop it from exploding.

"It was mean," said Jenna.

"I know. It was an awful thing to do," said Sukie.

"Unfortunately you were right about me. I was James's cheerleader."

"Was?" said Frannie.

"I broke up with him." Jenna dropped her purse and flopped backward on the spread. "Everything was about him." She threw out her arms. "He got so irritated because I called buffala mozzarella 'buff-a-*lo* mozzarella.' Then he was scandalized because I didn't know it really came from buffalos." She rolled over to face them. "Did you know that?"

Both Frannie and Sukie shook their heads.

"But from Italian buffalos, James said, which are more bovine. He actually used the word 'bovine.' What does it mean?"

"Cowlike," said Frannie.

"I can't be with someone who says 'bovine.' I can't be with someone who thinks mozzarella is more important than me."

"For sure," said Frannie.

"I can't be with someone who scolds me about cheese. I can't be with someone who's in love with himself."

"He reminds me of Léon," said Sukie.

"Léon?"

"The guy Madame Bovary flirts with in Yonville, who later breaks her heart. Léon was more interesting than any other man in Yonville, but not really interesting."

"You're right. James is Léon," said Jenna.

"When did this happen?" Frannie asked.

"An hour ago." Jenna popped up and looked at them brightly. When neither Sukie nor Frannie said anything, her shoulders sagged and her eyes wandered to an empty spot in the room.

"I told Frannie I was seeing this guy at Hudson Glen High. Actually I blabbed about him to everyone. But I'm not. He's not remotely into me. I made it up," said Sukie.

For some reason they all burst out laughing.

Sukie got the coziest feeling because they were all laughing together and not at anyone, and because they shared a wonderful giddiness that none of them could explain. Jenna stuffed her head into a pillow and Frannie clapped her hand over her mouth trying to stop. Sukie gave in to it, collapsing on the floor, loving how her body felt like jelly.

Sukie

SUKIE spent the night at Frannie's, and then the next. Frannie told her that her mom had checked in with Sukie's mom to let her know that Sukie was safe.

"Not that she cares," said Sukie.

Frannie had an unusual bathtub raised up off the floor. It had feet. "Claw feet," Frannie said they were called. They did look like the feet of a giant bird. Sukie spent an hour each night monopolizing it, doing the mermaid float.

On the third night, when Sukie was feeling especially relaxed, lounging in Frannie's terry-cloth robe with a towel wrapped around her wet hair, Frannie said, "You'd better tell us."

"What?" said Sukie.

"Why you're miserable and angry," said Jenna.

"I know all about being miserable and angry," said Frannie. "I fought with everyone for months after my dad died. I hated everyone."

"She did. Even me," said Jenna.

"How come?" said Sukie.

Frannie chewed some of her hair, realized what she was doing, and brushed the hair out of her mouth. "I'm trying to stop that." She laughed. "Let me think."

"What I mean," said Sukie, "is I hated everyone too, and I needed them to hate me but I don't know why. If I'm so smart, why don't I know why I do anything?"

"Who knows why they do anything?" said Jenna. "Is that some sort of cosmic question?"

"No, it's just—"

"I think it works like this," said Frannie. "You feel so awful, you need to feel worse, or you need to make it worse, or you need everyone else to feel awful. The point is, it spreads all over the place. I don't know why, but it does."

"A feel-awful epidemic," said Sukie. "That's what I've been living in." For a second she got excited at the idea, it sounded almost romantic. "Is that why you invited me to see that bird?"

"The hawk?" said Frannie. "It wasn't there and it was freezing; you're lucky you didn't come, but yes, when I saw you . . . well, whenever I saw you at school, I thought, Been there, done that. You're so unhappy."

"I really am." Sukie tried to smile but couldn't manage it.

"Come on, out with it. Burying it only makes it worse."

Sukie tried to think how to begin. She sat on the rug and picked at it. She searched the room as if the way to start were printed on the walls or hanging from the ceiling, or the moon whose bright whiteness peeped through the pine outside Frannie's window might guide her. Eventually her eyes settled on the fish drawing of Frannie's. The fish was driving. The fish had no hands, but there it was behind the wheel doing the impossible. She considered hiding in one of her voices—the squeaky baby one might gain more sympathy, the sophisticated drawl might dilute their pity, but she had lost the inclination to fakery. She knew that everything would become more real if she said it aloud. These sleepovers at Frannie's had been a vacation from pain, but she'd left Mikey and Señor.

Thank God for Señor, he would take good care of her brother, but still, Mikey needed her. Telling was the beginning of the journey home.

Sukie's voice broke as she started but steadied as she stuck to the facts and didn't embellish. "My mom found out my dad's involved with someone . . ." Sukie backtracked, forcing herself to say it. ". . . involved with another woman. She read it in my journal."

"She read your journal?" said Jenna.

"Shussh," said Frannie.

"She blamed me and threw me out. She threw him out too, I guess. I think they're getting a divorce." She covered her face with her hands.

Sukie rested a second, blinking into darkness. She wanted to get through this without the jumps. She lowered her hands, testing her calm. "I saw him with her. I was getting a mochaccino, and I turned . . . He didn't see me. He doesn't know. It's been my secret."

Sukie pulled the towel off her head and let the wet strands fall onto her shoulders. "I only saw them from the back. And heard him. I didn't get a good look."

As she worked up the energy to continue, she tapped her mouth nervously, and then said, "This is probably bad for me."

"What is?" said Jenna.

"My mom would say something like, 'Don't bat your lips, they'll flatten.' Can lips flatten? Is that even possible?" She laughed mirthlessly. "You know what my mom calls cellulite? Her 'shadows.' 'Don't look at my shadows,' she says. If I'm not calming her down or trying to please my dad, I don't know who I am."

Frannie reached over and squeezed Sukie's arm.

Sukie was beginning to think that Frannie knew more about feelings than anyone she had ever met. She listened in the most intense, unwavering way, but without an ounce of judgment. All confidences were safe, and for the first time Sukie felt that she wasn't carrying around a seven-hundred-pound burden. God, secrets could simply do you in. For a fleeting instant she wondered if Frannie had been as sympathetic as this before her dad died—Sukie had never known Frannie well enough to know that. Had tragedy softened her heart and heightened her sensors? Possibly, thought Sukie. Did that mean that tragedy could be a good thing—well, not good, exactly, but with a few positive side effects?

"I was frightened about everything after my dad died," Frannie told her, intuiting that the question was there. "But Simon helped a lot. He's fearless."

"What about me?" said Jenna. "Didn't I help?"

"You're always perfect," said Frannie.

Sukie knew what she meant. Jenna's cheerfulness and loyalty were necessary, like food.

Sukie scrambled up, dug her wallet out of her purse, and showed them the scrap of paper. "I think this is the woman's phone number. The other woman. I copied it out of my dad's BlackBerry. The number was there a whole bunch of times."

"Did you call it?" asked Frannie.

Sukie shook her head. "Should I?"

With their heads together, they scrutinized the little scrap of paper.

"Maybe I should burn it," said Sukie.

"We need to eat. We need to go out and eat. After we eat, we'll know," said Frannie. She got up and stretched. "I'm really sorry about your dad."

Sukie's face fell.

Frannie and Jenna exchanged looks as tears welled up and streamed down Sukie's cheeks. They put out their arms and swallowed her in a three-way hug.

"It's okay to cry about your dad," said Frannie.

"Not my dad," Sukie sobbed. "Yours." She broke

from the huddle and tried to catch her breath. "*Your* dad. I never told you I was sorry about *your* dad, and now you tell me you're sorry about *mine*." She erupted in a fresh wail.

"It's okay," said Frannie.

"No, it's not." Sukie sagged helplessly. "I meant to. Every day I meant to, but I didn't. I'm really, really sorry about your dad."

Frannie's eyes teared. Jenna looked at both of them and teared up too.

"Thanks," said Frannie, sniffling.

"You're welcome." Sukie collapsed in a chair. As she sat there silently, all the tears that hadn't flowed after she'd seen her dad that night, tears from the weight of carrying around the secret, tears from her loneliness and her mother's cruelty and for not telling Frannie she was sorry when such an awful thing had happened to her poured out. They kept coming and coming and coming. Finally she managed some words. "We'd better eat or I'll never stop."

Clementi's

INSTEAD of five minutes, it took twenty to get to Clementi's because Jenna, who had just gotten her license, refused to make left turns. They were too scary. She drove around the parking lot three times hunting for a diagonal spot with no cars on either side. By the time Jenna had managed to park crookedly, taking up two spaces, Sukie had forgotten her tears, and they were nearly doubled over with giggles. Then, instead of turning off the headlights, Jenna turned on the windshield wipers. In high spirits, they bounced into Clementi's.

All three girls had been coming here for pizza since they were kids, but only Sukie was a regular. Bunched up in front, a crowd of people waited for tables. Sukie craned over them. "Where's Issy? You'll love her. She told me, 'If I had a little sister, I'd want her to be you,' isn't that sweet? We're going to go shopping. She has the greatest taste. Oh there she is."

Isabella, in conversation with a couple at a back table, caught sight of Sukie waving, and raised a finger to indicate she'd be right there.

Sukie loved it here, the toasty pizza smell, the warmth of the coal-fire oven, Dominick, the owner, in a big white apron, who still came in now and then to make the pies himself at the marble counter, just as he had when she was little. She looked over at the bar, at the framed photos of Frank Sinatra—"a famous singer," her dad had told her. "This guy had class." He'd lifted her up so she could get a good view of a man with a wide, easy smile, looking suave in a pencil-thin black suit. "Class," he whispered in her ear. When they got home, he'd played her his music, which he'd explained was smooth and syncopated, cool and romantic.

"Sukie." Isabella tapped her shoulder.

"Issy." Sukie spun and threw her arms around her. Frannie and Jenna could see Issy's surprise, the knitted brow, the awkward way she patted Sukie on the back. "I'm sorry," said Sukie, letting go, stepping back, wiping her eyes with the back of her hand. "I didn't expect . . . It was seeing you and Sinatra." She lowered her voice to a whisper, "My parents might be getting a divorce." The tears squeezed out again.

"Oh. Oh, dear." Issy's delicate hands danced up and she clapped them together. Sukie could see she was at a loss. "Look, you guys, take this table, no one will notice." She scooted them to a booth in the back. "So here." She distributed menus.

"Have you seen him?" asked Sukie.

"Seen him?"

"Has my dad been here?"

"Yes, two days ago. Was it two days ago? Yes, two days ago."

"Alone?" asked Sukie.

Issy fussed with her hair, which was now a palomino blond, stabbing it with a clip. "He sat at the bar and watched the game."

"Did he say anything?"

"About what?"

"You know, the situation."

"No. Not a thing. What do you guys want to drink?"

"Diet Cokes," they all said at once. "With double

lemon," said Sukie. "It's great that way," she told Frannie and Jenna.

"Okay, I'll get the waitress. You're probably starved," said Issy.

"How's Richie?"

"Long gone. I've got to get back to work. Three Diet Cokes, six lemon slices."

Sukie examined the rolls in the bread basket, wondering where her dad was staying and if he was with the black-haired lady.

"What are you having?" asked Frannie.

"What?" said Sukie.

"Pizza or pasta?"

"Pizza."

"I think I'll have a salad," said Jenna.

"Salad. Boo," said Frannie.

"Dancers can't pig out," Jenna protested. "Oh, okay, I'll have plain pizza. A good old margherita."

While wolfing pizza, they discussed how great it would be to study in New York City next summer. Frannie at the Art Institute, Jenna at City Ballet, and Sukie . . . Sukie was stumped. "I have no idea what I want to be," said Sukie. "I used to think CEO, but I never knew of what. What could I do there?" Frannie and Jenna threw out all sorts of suggestions—interning at a law firm or online for a website, modeling, maybe they need assistants at the big tennis tournament, the US Open. They discussed what was sexy in a guy, and Frannie announced that she'd once been fixated on the frayed cuff of Simon's shirt. "There is nothing sexier than a shirt disintegrating," she said. Sukie confided about going to Bobo's game and getting stuck in the mud and the giant hawk mascot nearly suffocating her, and everyone was groaning and laughing. "Mister le Bobo," Frannie nicknamed him.

While they were sharing a hot-fudge sundae and Jenna swore, while she licked her spoon, that if she took even one more mouthful she'd be a dancing cow, Sukie laid down the scrap of paper. They tried to decide again.

"Spin a fork," said Frannie. "If it points toward you, you call. Anywhere else, no."

Sukie spun the fork. It flew off the table.

"That doesn't count," said Frannie, retrieving it. "Spin the knife."

Around it went twice and slid into Sukie's lap.

"Oh, no."

"You've got to do it," said Frannie.

Sukie toyed with her cell, letting her fingers play over the numbers. "It's probably a bank. Probably just related to some business deal he was making, right?"

"Right," said Jenna.

She dialed and pressed the phone against her ear. She could barely hear the ring. She pressed her fingers against her other ear to blot out the noise.

She clicked off, sat down, and dropped her cell on the table as if it were radioactive.

"What happened?" said Jenna.

"A bank or a woman?" said Frannie.

"A woman. She said, 'Hello.'"

"Uh-oh," said Jenna.

"That's it for me." Sukie dug into the sundae. Her cell vibrated. She glanced over. "Oh my God, it's the number. The bitch is calling back."

Sukie pushed the phone away, into the center of the table. Every time it vibrated, it moved.

"It's alive," said Frannie.

Sukie snatched it and pressed the green button, "Yes," she said.

"Did you just try to call me? I didn't recognize the number." The squeaky, scratchy voice was unmistakable.

Sukie twisted in the booth. At the back computer, Issy had her cell to her ear.

"Issy?" said Frannie.

"That's impossible," said Jenna. "Isn't that impossible?"

Sukie's scalp prickled. She was on fire.

With a shrug of her shoulders, Issy slid the phone into her back pocket and went into the kitchen.

"She's like three years older than you," said Jenna.

"More like eight," said Frannie, "but still."

Sukie sprang up, dodged a waiter, split a family of six making their stuffed way to the front, and barged past Dominick and into the kitchen, where Issy was popping a chef hat off a cook.

"My dad," said Sukie.

Issy gave the chef back his hat. "What about him?"

"Did you see *The Other Boleyn Girl*?"

Issy walked past the giant refrigerators, the boxes of sodas and cans of tomatoes. She smacked the steel door, opening it. Sukie stormed after her into the parking lot, with Frannie and Jenna in her wake. "Was your hair black? Did you dye your hair black?"

"Why?"

"You did."

"Maybe. So? It wasn't anything." She kept walking.

Sukie slapped her arm to stop her. "What wasn't anything?"

"Maybe it meant something to your dad. It was nice for a while, he's still into me, but I told him, hey, I'm like in between, I'm not ending up here. I'm considering my options. You're like sixty."

"My dad's not sixty," Sukie shouted.

"Okay, forty, whatever, calm down. What's the difference?" She bent to primp in a side mirror. She fluffed her hair, ran her tongue over her teeth, applied some gloss. "Men like me," she said with a shrug.

"Issy, we were friends."

"Who?"

"You and I."

"Not really."

"Not really! I can't believe you're saying that."

"You're a customer."

"A customer? I confided in you," said Sukie. "You invited me shopping. You said if you had a sister you'd want her to be me."

"When did I say that?"

"I was in the bathroom and—" Sukie stopped.

"The bathroom?" Issy eyed her curiously, truly baffled.

Frannie and Jenna, whose heads had been whipping back and forth as they followed the arguments, instinctively closed in behind Sukie, correctly intuiting from her strange expression, the slight swaying, and an uncontrollable blink that she was in danger of toppling. She might need catching.

"I don't have a clue what you're talking about," said Issy.

"It's really freezing out. I'm freezing," said Sukie. She started forward, backed up, turned. Frannie and Jenna, flanking her, steered her back into Clementi's.

Nobody spoke on the way home. In the backseat Sukie was lost in thought. Issy wasn't her friend. She was her friend in the mirror. Sukie had invented her and, judging from everything she'd seen and learned tonight, she hadn't invented even a reasonable facsimile.

"Do you think you can cause something to happen just from wanting it so much?" she asked.

"I don't get what you mean. Does this have to do with your dad?" asked Frannie.

"Not really. I'm talking about loneliness."

Frannie turned around and considered her answer. For a while she seemed to be in a wilderness of her own. "Do you mean that you imagined that Issy was your friend?"

"Yes, so completely that it was real."

"Oh that can happen. I believe that totally. Loneliness is powerful."

Mirror Confessions

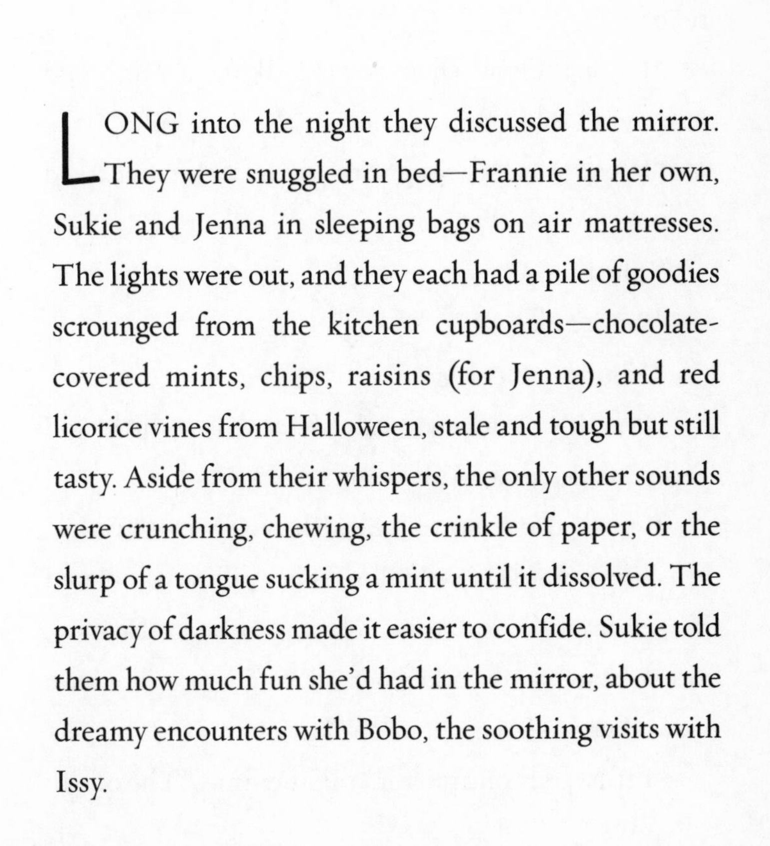

LONG into the night they discussed the mirror. They were snuggled in bed—Frannie in her own, Sukie and Jenna in sleeping bags on air mattresses. The lights were out, and they each had a pile of goodies scrounged from the kitchen cupboards—chocolate-covered mints, chips, raisins (for Jenna), and red licorice vines from Halloween, stale and tough but still tasty. Aside from their whispers, the only other sounds were crunching, chewing, the crinkle of paper, or the slurp of a tongue sucking a mint until it dissolved. The privacy of darkness made it easier to confide. Sukie told them how much fun she'd had in the mirror, about the dreamy encounters with Bobo, the soothing visits with Issy.

"Everything was so much nicer in the mirror," she said.

"Nicer than what?" said Jenna.

"Than my life. Except sometimes."

She told them about the freaky wicked turns—her butt as big as an island, her ramp a four-lane highway.

"What ramp?" said Frannie.

"The ramp down my nose. The one my mother got rid of."

"I don't know what you're talking about," said Frannie. "I'd kill for your nose."

"Why? What's wrong with *your* nose?" Jenna asked Frannie.

"The bump."

"But it's elegant."

"A bump isn't elegant."

"It is, it's positively regal. My nose is so little and perky," said Jenna. "Who wants perky?"

It turned out no one liked her own nose. Sukie, brushing potato chip crumbs off her pillow, wondered if spending all that time relating to her reflection, rather than, say, another person, might possibly have blown her anxieties out of proportion.

"I trust only one mirror," said Frannie. "The one in

the downstairs bathroom. If I'm going out, that's the one I look in."

"Why is that?" asked Jenna.

"I don't know. Maybe it's the light, maybe it's the mirror, maybe it's me."

"My grandmother's mirror is especially flattering," said Sukie. "Except when it isn't."

"Sometimes," said Jenna, "when I'm in dance class, I go nearly mad looking in the mirror. I see my thighs, only my thighs, nothing else, and they look simply huge, especially compared to Cecelia's thighs. She dances next to me. If you watch yourself in the mirror, you can't dance. I mean, you can but not really because you're supposed to let go, to feel the music and the movement, and yet how in the world am I expected to do that with all those mirrors?"

"Your thighs are perfect," said Sukie. "I'd love to have your graceful ballet legs."

"Remember when Mom forced me to play soccer?" said Frannie.

"You hated it," said Jenna.

"I was on that team," said Sukie.

"Right, you were. You were good, but the coach, Coach Randall McCord, I remember his whole name, it's burned in my brain because he was really mean to me. I'd be daydreaming in the middle of practice and the ball would go right by or hit me on the head, and he would scream. He called me Flake."

"I vaguely remember that," said Sukie.

"'Hey, Flake, wake up.' 'Hey everyone, look at Flake.' 'Hey Flake, run around the track ten times.' I'd come home, lock myself in the bathroom, and tell him off in the mirror. I would call him much worse names than Flake." Frannie giggled. "Then I would say, 'You are arrested for extreme mental and physical cruelty and are going straight to jail.' It really helped, it did, it helped."

"Who used to sing in the mirror, raise her hand?" said Jenna.

They all raised their hands.

"What about with a hairbrush for a microphone?"

They all kept their hands up.

Sukie sat up and pulled the sleeping bag around her shoulders to keep warm. "I have to tell you something strange. My mirror cracked. I feel as if I caused it because it didn't just crack, it kind of cracked up. But that's impossible. I researched it. Telekinesis has no basis in science. That a person can cause an object to move or change . . . that energy, grief, or I guess joy or anxiety or even fierce determination could cause something to happen . . . people claim to have done it, but there's no proof at all."

"Just because you can't prove something scientifically," said Frannie, "doesn't mean it's not possible. Things happened to me—"

"Things?"

"After my dad died," said Frannie.

She left it at that, and the silence that followed was deep, like the quiet of deep sleep. Sukie knew not to pry further.

"You lived in that mirror more than you lived in the real world," said Frannie.

"It's true," said Sukie.

"So."

Dad

THE next morning when Sukie was eating French toast in the most delicious way, with sour cream and blueberry jam, and Frannie's mother was fretting about how many more poinsettia plants to order for the Christmas season, the doorbell rang.

"Your dad's here, Sukie," Mel called.

"You don't have to see him," said Frannie, "does she, Mom?"

Sukie looked pleadingly at Frannie's mom as her dad came into the kitchen. He didn't put out his arms as he normally would and expect her to fly into them. All he said was "Hi, kiddo." He didn't mosey around to investigate his surroundings and lay on the compliments or probe Mel about his work or Frannie's mom about the flower business. He pulled out a chair at the breakfast table and sat down next to his daughter. "How about some tennis?"

"It's twelve degrees out," said Sukie.

"Not quite. More like forty. I brought your racket and sweats. It will be fun."

In the car Sukie kept her eyes directed out the side window. She counted out-of-state license plates, a game she and Mikey used to play, but the thing about riding in cars is that eventually you talk. There is too much history, going for ice cream, being picked up from school or taken to the movies. Or, as her dad was doing right now, driving to the club. Sukie and her dad had ridden together too many times and shared too many confidences on those car trips not to end up talking now.

After a few blocks of quiet, her dad jumped to the heart of the matter.

"Look," he said, "I'd like to tell you that I'm a good guy, that your mom and I are back on track, and that your life is going to be easy, but I think what I have to be with you is honest. I don't know what's in store."

"Are you and mom getting divorced?"

"We don't know. Your mom and I lost our way.

You know, she's difficult and—"

"Stop," said Sukie. "Stop right there, Dad. Don't criticize Mom to me. I don't want you to do that anymore even though . . . well, I just don't."

"Fair enough," he said.

"That guy called you slime."

"What guy?"

"The one who punched you."

"Richie?"

"That was Richie?" said Sukie. "That was Issy's boyfriend?"

"He's a hothead." Her dad pulled over and let the car idle. He drummed his thumb on the steering wheel. "I'm sorry that happened. I'm sorry you went through that, and all of this."

"Is he right? Are you slime?"

"What do you think?"

Sukie shook her head. "I don't know what to think."

"Your mom wants to see you."

"No way," said Sukie.

"I know she booted you out, but she went a little crazy when she found out . . ." Sukie could see that it took great effort but he forced himself not to hedge.

" . . . when she found out about me and Isabella."

"I'll never forgive her."

"I hope you do," said her dad. "I hope you'll forgive us both."

"Are you living at the house now?"

"No, but nothing is settled." He started up the car again and pulled into traffic. "God, I miss tennis, don't you? I can't wait to see that killer forehand of yours."

"Do you know if Mom happened to notice Grandma's mirror?" asked Sukie.

"She didn't say anything. Why?"

"It cracked. It cracked a million ways from Sunday."

"How?"

"Stress," said Sukie.

Back

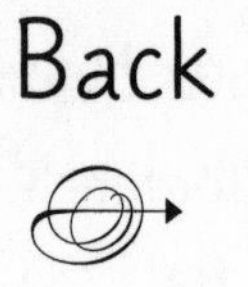

MIKEY tore down the stairs and threw himself at Sukie. When she half carried, half dragged her brother back upstairs because he simply would not let go, Señor came to greet her at the top. He brushed against Sukie's legs, circling around and around, rubbing against her.

"Hi, my darling beast." She knelt and hugged him, pressing her face into his fur, inhaling the musty scent of a dog seriously in need of a bath.

She tapped the door to her room and let it swing slowly and soundlessly open. After the comforting mess of Frannie's bedroom, with its collage of personal expression on the walls, display of bizarre objects, rumpled spread with an ink stain, her own neat and pretty environment seemed the room of a stranger. She sat on the edge of the bed and bounced gently, reacquainting herself with it.

Her mother bustled in, setting down a vase with some pink baby roses in it. "A homecoming," she said. "I picked up some tacos for lunch, the ones with chicken, your favorite."

She fussed with the buds, pulling the roses this way and that. Her hair, normally exquisitely coiffed, appeared egg-beaten in the back. She'd obviously brushed the front that morning and, either from loss of focus or despair, had forgotten to do the rest of it. When she finally turned, she couldn't quite meet Sukie's eye. Her face, bright thanks to an application of full makeup, still had shadows of sleeplessness. Her blush was too bright and sharply drawn. She hadn't blended. Since her mom was big on blending and had held forth on the subject on many occasions, Sukie knew that her mom was a wreck.

Already, within seconds of seeing her, Sukie felt more sorry for her mom than she did for herself.

"Oh yes, I also got that cake you love, the yellow with the pink frosting. I might even have some."

There would be no apology, Sukie realized. Flowers,

tacos, and cake were the closest her mother could come.

It was a perfect time to break the news. Her mom was vulnerable. She was feeling guilty, albeit without the courage or grace to meet the problem head-on, nevertheless she was trying to inch into Sukie's good graces while overwhelmed with her own marital problems. She'd never have the energy or inclination now to pitch a fit, and Sukie did not have the tiniest twinge of guilt in taking advantage of that.

"Grandmother's mirror," said Sukie. "I've been meaning to show you."

She walked into the bathroom. Her mother followed.

"Oh, dear," her mom said as she and Sukie beheld their distorted reflections in the splintered glass. "It's literally gone to pieces. I've never heard of anything like this, of a mirror disintegrating like a natural disaster. I've seen spots on old mirrors, mottling like the skin on old people's hands, but this? It has to go."

"Does it?" said Sukie.

The mirror had reflected every turn her mind took, every anxiety, every wish, every vanity, and it had cracked under the strain, she had no doubt about it. For good and bad it reflected her soul, and that made it, in some true way, a living thing.

How could she get rid of it?

She was even frightened to get rid of it.

How could she keep it?

"Should we save the frame?" said her mom. "Or see if an antique dealer wants it? Is it actually silver? It could be pewter or even steel. Maybe we should simply cart it to the sidewalk and let the garbage men take it." Her mom rubbed her back against the doorjamb. "I have an itch and I'm practicing for when I'm alone. I mean if your dad and I don't . . ." She faltered. "Well, it's not a big problem, it's just I've been thinking about all of it, large and small."

"Maybe Señor could learn to scratch you. He's good at scratching himself."

They smiled and, in the broken mirror, four broken smiles came back at them.

Her mother stroked the frame. "It's useless now."

"Which means . . . ," said Sukie. "Do you know what that means?"

"What?"

"It's art."

Art

"FRANNIE'S here," called Sukie's mom.

Sukie stuck her head over the banister and waved her up.

"Where is this thing?" said Frannie as Sukie's phone rang.

"Here, this way, in the bathroom. Hello. It's Jenna," she told Frannie. "She's parking. She's getting out of the car, she's walking up the front walk, she's ringing the doorbell."

The doorbell rang.

"It's Jenna, for me," called Sukie.

"Hi," said Jenna, walking in and shrugging off her parka. "Sukie's expecting me."

"Well, sure." Her mom was smiling as widely as

her face work could ever permit. "Go right on up."

Sukie and Frannie lifted the mirror off the bathroom wall and, with Jenna directing and Mikey and Señor getting in the way, carried it into Sukie's bedroom and laid it on a large piece of plastic spread over the carpet.

Sukie banged the tin of metal polish and pried off the top. "I figure we have to polish the frame."

"We could distress it too," said Frannie.

"What does that mean?" asked Sukie.

"After you shine it, you buff it with steel wool. It makes for a great effect."

"Let's definitely do that." Sukie handed out special soft polishing cloths and read the directions aloud. "Rub gently."

They flopped on the floor and got to work.

"I've been thinking," said Sukie. "We can't hang it in the bathroom again, because then it's still just a mirror. Environment is important."

"That is so true," said Frannie, "especially with art."

"And it shouldn't be vertical because that's also its normal way of being. Diagonal would be cool, but impossible to hang, so horizontal." Sukie was bubbling with originality. "And over there, that's where it goes." She pointed to the wall above her desk. "By the way, do you want popcorn? Mikey will get it, won't you?"

Mikey, draped over the bed, rolled off. "What kind do you want?" he asked.

"Just butter and salt for me," said Sukie.

"Butter and salt, the only way," said Frannie.

"Butter and salt," said Jenna. "That must be why we're all friends. James was always forcing me to have popcorn with truffle oil." She fell silent as she rubbed more polish onto the frame, unaware that she had said the thing that Sukie had been hoping with her whole heart was true.

Until that moment she hadn't been certain. Did Frannie and Jenna really like her or were they being kind because they felt sorry for her? Now, dropped into the conversation so casually as if it were self-evident, the fact: They were friends. Sukie finally had friends, great ones. Loyal, soulful, fun. What more could she ask?

Late that night she wrote in her journal that today was maybe the happiest of her life, and, with all that was going on with her parents, how strange was that?

She patted Señor. "In a second I'll turn out the light, but I have to finish. Besides, you're in it."

Selecting a turquoise Sharpie—turquoise being, in her opinion, the color of joy—she wrote: *Just as we were done distressing the frame, Simon arrived. Señor, who observes all newcomers from afar, bolted down the stairs and danced around Simon. Simon dropped right down on the marble floor—Mom nearly had kittens—and they rolled around together. Simon turns out to be the only person in the world around whom Señor behaves like a dog.*

After we agreed that the placement was perfect, and that really did take time and patience, Simon banged a nail into the wall and hung the mirror. Frannie, Jenna, and I jumped on the bed. That way we were all tall enough to greet our reflections. Jenna demonstrated ballet moves while the mirror fractured them. We swayed and watched ourselves crack into pieces, our eyes multiply, our legs split, our arms separate from our bodies, our hair appear to float. All in all, it was thrilling.

Sukie closed her journal and tucked it into the drawer in her bedside table, thinking that she'd find a serious hiding place tomorrow. She clicked off the light.

"Good night, Señor." She kissed his wet nose, pulled up the covers, and, comfortably squished into the sliver of space that the dog allotted her, fell instantly asleep.

Acknowledgments

I couldn't have written this book without Maia Harari's remarkable research or without the frankness, honesty, and generosity of Jane Weiss. I can never write any book without the emotional wisdom of my husband, Jerome Kass, or the guidance of my close friend Lorraine Bodger. Jill Santopolo, my editor, has my deepest gratitude for her talent and sensitivity. Her contribution was essential and so appreciated, and she makes everything more fun, which is no small thing. Working with her is a joy.